NO TIME FOR DETOURS

NO BRIDES CLUB, BOOK 9

JEAN C. GORDON

Upstate NY Romance

ISBN-13: 978-1-7321836-7-4

No Time for Detours

© 2020, Jean C. Gordon

Cover Design by RockSolidBookDesign.com
Proofread by Alice Shepherd

This is a work of fiction. Names, characters, organizations, places, events, and incidents are either products of the author's imagination or are used fictitiously. Any resemblance to actual persons, living or dead, or actual events is purely coincidental.

Sweet Promise Press
PO Box 72
Brighton, MI 48116

Dedicated to Caroline and Josh and their twins who inspired this story.

And, as always, thanks to my critique group BFF (Chris, Colleen, and Thomasine) and my editor Jena O'Connor.

What's our Sweet Promise? It's to deliver the heart-warming, entertaining, clean, and wholesome reads you love with every single book.

From contemporary to historical romances to suspense and even cozy mysteries, all of our books are guaranteed to put a song in your heart and a smile on your face. That's our promise to you, and we can't wait to deliver upon it...

We release one new book per week, which means the flow of sweet, relatable reads coming your way never ends. Make sure to save some space on your eReader!

———

Check out our books in Kindle Unlimited at
sweetpromisepress.com/Unlimited

Pre-order upcoming series bundles to save at
sweetpromisepress.com/Shop

Join our reader discussion group, meet our authors,
and make new friends at
sweetpromisepress.com/Group

Sign up for our weekly newsletter at
sweetpromisepress.com/Subscribe

And don't forget to like us on Facebook at
sweetpromisepress.com/FB

1

I did it! A horn honking pulled Ava Lewis's attention to the window of her apartment complex. She looked at the cars and pedestrians humming along Broadway and Murray Street in the Tribeca area of New York City. Her city now. *Just as I planned.* And despite the skepticism of her family—except her older sister Kate.

"Ms. Ava, we finished our pictures."

Ava spun around toward the five-year-old twins, a girl and a boy sitting at the art table of the Kids Korner. Where her attention should have been instead of on the city outside.

Make that going *almost* as she'd planned. So far, the only work the three temp agencies she'd signed with had gotten her was substitute preschool teacher/childcare jobs, not the law office work she wanted. She'd thought she was done with childcare when she'd left Genesee Head Start in Western New York.

"Good job, Mia and Lucas." She smiled and looked at the clock. Five o'clock. Time for the Jansen Athletic Club's Kiddie Korner to close for the dinner hour and her shift to be over. "And your mother should be done with her Tai Chi class, too." Should have been finished a half hour ago.

"Kitchen's clean." Louisa, the aide that had been working with Ava entered the playroom.

"Thanks. You can go ahead home. I'll wait for the kids' mother."

"Okay. If you turn the lever on the inside of the door, it will lock when you close it," Louisa said. "It was nice working with you. Maybe I'll see you again."

"The same." *But you won't see me here again if I can help it.*

Ava waited another five minutes. She was supposed to meet her sister and her friends, the members of the No Brides Club, at the Briarwood Tavern at five-thirty. Ava had been looking forward to it since Kate had invited her. She opened the file cabinet and pulled out the form Louisa had had the kids' mother fill out.

"While you put the crayons back in the box, I'm going to call your mother to check on when she's picking you up," Ava said, alert to any signs that either Mia or Lucas were uncomfortable that they were the only ones left in the Kiddie Korner. Neither appeared to be. Ava tried the phone number their mother had put on the form. The call went right to voicemail. She left a message and skimmed down the form for an alternate contact. *Bingo*. Nick Jansen, uncle, right here in the center's corporate business office.

"Come on kids." Ava took Mia's and Lucas's hands. "Your mom said to take you to your Uncle Nick."

"Yay!" Mia and Lucas shouted, with Lucas adding, "We haven't seed Uncle Nick in a long time."

Ava dropped their hands once they'd walked through the glass door to the hallway. "Stand right here with me while I lock up."

Lucas stood quietly beside her while Ava followed the instructions she'd gotten for locking up. Mia, on the other hand, twirled around a couple of times before spotting something of interest to her and starting across the hall.

Ava grabbled the little girl's shoulder with her left hand while she pulled the glass door closed with her right.

"Stay with me," Ava said mostly to Mia. "I have to stop at the front desk to find out where your uncle's office is."

"Hi, can I help you?" the woman at the front desk asked. It was a different person than the one who'd been there when Ava had started her shift.

"Yes, I'm looking for Nick Jansen's office."

After eyeing the twins, she answered, "That must be the accounting guy. Go down the hall to my right. The business office is the only thing on that hall. You can't miss it."

"Thanks." Ava's stomach knotted at the vagueness of the staff person's answer. She couldn't just leave the twins with anyone. But she didn't want to miss her meeting, and she wanted to change out of her jeans and t-shirt into something more professional looking.

She had no trouble finding the office and, despite the many desks she saw through the door window, only one was occupied. Ava knocked while the twins stood on tippy toes to look through the window.

"That's Uncle Nick," Mia said in a loud whisper.

Not to be outdone, Lucas said, "He works with numbers and stuff."

Ava recoiled, punched in the gut by the sight of the man at the desk. Medium athletic build, square chin, patrician nose, and broad shoulders. Except for his auburn-brown, slightly wavy hair, he looked like an older version of her ex-fiancé. She shook off her idiocy. She was over Trey, had been for a long time. Countless men in New York must have those same characteristics. No reason to hold her past against this guy.

"Let's surprise him," Mia said. Before Ava could stop her, Mia tugged down on the door lever, and she and Lucas pushed the door open.

———

"Uncle Nick!"

Nick Jansen looked up from the jumble of financial figures in the spreadsheet he had open on the computer in the corporate business office of Jansen Athletic Club, his uncle Pete's fitness club network. He was just wrapping up his first day of vetting the company's finances as a make-ready to sell it. Mia and Lucas, the four-, no five- now, year-old twins he hadn't seen in six months propelled themselves at him. What were they doing here?

"Hey, guys," he said hugging them close on his lap.

"Sorry."

His attention jumped to the petite, dark-haired woman following Mia and Lucas in. He generally preferred long hair on women, but her neat, pixie cut matched her no-nonsense expression and stance.

Mia pulled his shirt collar for his attention.

What was he doing, thinking about women's hair styles when he had a more pressing problem on his lap?

"Mommy said we'd get to see you," the little girl said.

"I didn't believe her," Lucas added.

One thing Nick had not loved about his ex-fiancée was that she had a compulsion to mislead the twins to get them to behave.

"Your sister?" the woman with the twins began.

"Ex-fiancée," Nick automatically answered.

The woman pursed her lips. "Their mother," she corrected herself, "put you down as an alternate contact if I needed to get hold of her. She was taking the 4:00 Tai Chi class and didn't come to pick them up."

Constance wasn't exactly the kids' mother. Nor was he their real uncle. But Constance was the twin's legal guardian, and they'd planned on adopting them once they'd married. She might have gone ahead with the adoption without him. But that was ancient history. Nick clicked on the center's class schedule he'd opened before he'd decided to tackle the spreadsheet. "That class ended more than thirty minutes ago." He closed the schedule. "You're from the childcare service, I take it?"

She straightened to her possibly full five foot four. "Yes, a temp, scheduled to work until 5:00, when I was instructed to close the Kiddie Korner."

Mia slid off his lap and wandered toward the fish tank on the other side of the office. Lucas followed.

He weighed whether there was any way Mia could knock over or break the tank. Things had a way of self-destructing when Mia was in a room. Nick decided it was unlikely, at least not in the amount of time it would take for him to finish with

... he didn't know the woman's name. He rose to follow the twins, just in case.

The woman extended her hand. "I'm Ava Lewis."

He shook her hand. "Nick Jansen."

"Yes, Uncle Nick," she said. Her face split into a grin that softened her features. "But before I can leave the twins, I'll need to see your ID."

"Of course." As he reached in his back pocket for his wallet, Nick followed Ava's gaze to the twins, who had their noses to the aquarium, getting awfully up close and personal with the few fish swimming away from their faces.

Mia reached to lift the top to the tank. Nick closed the distance between them. "Let's go find your mother." *And find out why you're here and how she found me.*

"O-kay." The little girl lowered her hand.

Nick removed his license from his wallet and handed it to Ava.

"Thanks." Ava handed his license back.

Nick put it away and took Mia's hand firmly in his, offering his other hand to Lucas.

"I guess my work is done," Ava said edging toward the door, as if anxious to escape him. Or more likely escape Mia. He didn't know how long the little girl had been in Ava's care, but it didn't take long to get Mia's number.

"Wait." Nick halted, not knowing exactly why he'd said that, except he didn't want Ava to leave. Time for some of that fast, decisive thinking he was known for. "I had a quick tour around the facility this morning, but I don't remember which room is the one where the Tai Chi class was."

This was true. One of the assistant managers had given him a walk around, and he didn't know where the Tai Chi classes were held. Although he could easily find out from the person on the front desk.

"Sorry, I don't know." Ava smiled.

Maybe he'd misread her off-putting tone before?

"Thanks, anyway."

Ava walked alongside them as he ushered the twins to the main lobby with Mia dancing around replaying a story Ava had read them. That cancelled any chance he had to talk with Ava. Not that there was any reason to talk to her. She'd given him all the info on the kids.

"See you," he said as Ava turned toward the front door, although there was little chance of that. She was a temp employee, and he wouldn't be here long either.

Ava waved bye to him and the twins.

Nick got the information he needed from the front desk and jogged after Mia and Lucas who were headed toward the stairs to the upper jogging deck.

"Whoa, guys. Not upstairs. We're looking for your mother down here." He put an arm firmly around each of their shoulders and herded them toward the room where the Tai Chi class had been held. It was dark with the door locked. "Stay right here next to me and see who can hop longer on one foot."

The twins were always up for a competition. He pulled his phone from his pocket and pressed the number he had for Constance.

"We're sorry, the number you called is out of service."

Nick punched end call. "Great."

"Us, Uncle Nick?" Lucas asked.

He glanced at the tow-headed boy hopping next to him. "Yep." Lucas was by far the more insecure of the two.

"Uncle Nick, you made me miss a hop," Mia complained

Change that to the only insecure one of the two.

"Do you guys know your mother's phone number?"

Over each other, they recited the number he had just called.

His stomach churned. "Come on, we have to check back at the desk to see where your mother is."

A different person was behind the desk.

"Can I help you?" she said.

Nick introduced himself and asked if she knew where he could find the Tai Chi instructor for the four o'clock class if he or she was still here.

"You're in luck. That's me."

While he liked what his uncle had said about all the staff chipping in to help where needed, the centers needed to have assigned coverage of the front desk, not just whoever might be available.

"The guest participant in your last class, a woman with long blonde hair—did she mention trying any of the other facilities?"

"I did the subtle cross-sell routine, but, no she didn't show an interest in anything else." The Tai Chi instructor eyed the twins. "Cute kids. Yours?"

Mia had ambled over to the wall and was pushing the buttons on the drink vending machine, while Lucas squatted at his feet inspecting a bug someone had crushed into the well-worn rug.

"No." He modulated his voice. "Thanks."

"Mia, get over here, please. Up, Lucas." Both kids

safe in hand, Nick headed toward the parking lot door. "Does Mommy still have the same car?"

"Nope," Mia said. "She got a new little blue one."

"An Accord Sport," Lucas added.

He opened a side door to the athletic club's assigned area in the attached parking garage and stepped out. He didn't see any blue Hondas among the few cars parked there.

Lucas was a little motorhead, but maybe he'd gotten the car make and model wrong. "Do you guys see Mommy's car?"

"Nope. It's at Carson's house," Mia tried to pull her hand from his.

"He's Mommy's boyfriend. He doesn't like kids like you do," Lucas said.

Nick drew a long breath. "In Philadelphia, where you live?"

"Nope, he moved to Texas," Mia said.

Nick wasn't even going to try to untangle that. "How did you guys get here?"

"Mommy rented an SUV to bring our stuff."

Lucas's words brought relief. There were three SUVs in the lot. "Is the SUV Mommy rented the silver one, the black one, or the white one?"

"None of them," Lucas answered. "It's red."

"You're sure?"

"Yes," Mia said in an exasperated tone. "We're five. We know our colors."

Nick looked to the garage ceiling and muttered. "Great. What am I going to do now?"

"Take us to your apartment," Mia said. "That's where we left our stuff."

"Yep," Lucas added. "Mommy said we're going to be staying with you now."

2

Ava burst from the elevator and rushed up the hall to the apartment she was "house" sitting for friends of her brother-in-law Jon. She'd swear the elevator had stopped to let people off or on at every floor between the first floor and the 22nd where the apartment was.

Once inside, she glanced at the DVR clock. 5:20. The No Brides Club was meeting at 5:30 several blocks away. But she *had to* shower and change. Ava texted her sister that she was running late, adding that she'd had to work late to stave off any comment from Kate about her always being late. That was the old Ava. Besides, didn't professional women have to work late a lot?

She jumped in and out of the shower, glad for

her recent decision to have her shoulder-length hair cut in a quick-to-manage style. A pang of doubt struck her when she looked at her towel dried hair in the mirror. She'd always worn her hair long. Kate hadn't seen her since she'd had it cut. Nothing she could do about that now. She blow-dried it in a couple minutes, went to the bedroom, and pulled a simple belted wrap dress with flutter sleeves in black and white checks from the closet. Summery but still acceptable business attire. She redid her makeup and slipped on black double strap sandals with a block heel that would make her power walk to the Briarwood easier.

Ava was glad for the air conditioning when she walked into the Briarwood's dining area. While Kate had said they often met in the roof-top bar, the group was meeting in the dining room tonight for dinner. They weren't hard to spot, sitting at one of the large corner tables with tufted leather banquette seating. Especially with her sister standing and waving with one hand while pointing to her own hair with the other.

Ava stopped by the bar and ordered a Long Island iced tea, because she'd never had one before, and to give herself another minute to calm her excitement at meeting Kate's friends. These women

were who she wanted to be in a few years—
successful and not boring, as Trey had said she'd
become when he broke their engagement. She
sipped the drink. *Not bad.* Then took another sip. *Not
bad at all.* Fortified, she marched across the room.

"Ava," Kate stood and said when she'd gotten
within conversation distance. "I love your hair." Kate
looked over her shoulder at the seated women. "Ava's
had long hair ever since she was small."

"Thanks. I panicked the first time I looked in the
mirror at the apartment after I'd gotten it cut. But I
like it, too." Ava stopped herself from adding that it
was great today when she was rushing around
getting changed and ready to come here. These were
women who naturally would have already dressed
for success.

"Sit down and I'll introduce you to everyone."
Kate pulled out the chair next to her at the table, and
Ava sat.

"I'll start with Kinsley and Julie, who I've told
you all about. They're the only other original No
Brides Club members who could make it today."

"Hi." Ava reached for her drink. *Yeah.* As she
knew, Kinsley King was a top real estate broker in
the city and managed a wildlife sanctuary upstate
and Julie Harrison was a software developer and

Kate's college friend. Both of them, like her sister, were now married and emeritus members of the club. Ava took a slug of her tea. And her sister was one of the small percent of mutual fund managers who were women.

"Then there's our newer members, Emelie Sullivan, Vivian Hart, Brooke Collins, Marnie Bates, Julie's cousin Samantha Dennis, and Lizzie Sullivan. "This is my sister Ava, who's on her way to becoming the club's first attorney-member."

"Nice to meet you," Ava said, keeping her glass within easy reach. They were inviting her to join?

Kate continued, "Emelia and her twin are the number one wedding planners in NYC. Brooke is a pediatric oncology nurse at Children's Hospital."

Ava curved her fingers around her drink.

"Marnie is a TV producer."

Ava lifted the glass to her lips and took a mouthful.

"Vivian is a third-grade teacher from Northern Virginia, who's apartment-sitting for her great aunt for the summer, and Samantha is working as a bartender, but is a paralegal by training."

Ava swallowed, and the tea went down smoothly. A couple people she had things in common with. "Vivian, I'm a former preschool teacher and am apartment sitting for friends of Kate's husband, who are on sabbatical this summer."

"We'll have to trade teacher notes sometime," Vivian said with a warm smile.

Ava smiled back. She'd only taught full time for a year. She didn't know how many notes she had to trade.

"And as Kate inferred, I'm a law student, pursuing dual Juris Doctor and Masters in Social Work degrees at NYU." Or she would be as long as she got through the summer program for new law students who didn't have an undergraduate degree in pre-law. Hers was in early childhood education. Not exactly the stuff to impress.

"So you're almost right around the corner," Kinsley said. "You should have no trouble getting to meetings."

Ava polished off her drink. They *were* inviting her to become part of the group.

"The group's main rules are that you're totally dedicated to your career goal to the exclusion of dating, marriage, and any other outside influence that could detour you from that goal. And because the members are here to support each other, you need to make it to the Thursday evening meetings as often as possible," Kinsley explained.

Ava nodded, along with some of the other newer members. After devoting much of her high school and college social life to being with Trey, only for him to break their engagement almost before it got started, she'd have no trouble foregoing men for a while—a long while. A picture of Nick Jansen with his square chin and chiseled cheekbones flashed in her mind. She blinked it away as an effect of drinking her Long Island iced tea too fast on an empty stomach.

"Of course, as you know from your sister and me, Ava, foregoing men and marriage isn't a lifetime vow. It's only until you achieve your career goals. Now who's ready to order dinner?" Kinsley asked.

After food and another iced tea, Ava's nerves about being accepted by her sister's significantly older—thirty-something—friends had calmed considerably. She walked out of the tavern with Kate.

"Call me any time for anything," Kate said. "New York City isn't Genesee, you know."

And I'm twenty-three, not thirteen, Ava said silently. "I'm fine. You were only eighteen when you moved to New York City for college."

Kate's mouth opened, but no words came out.

"Right. I have to stop thinking of you as my baby sister."

"You've got it." Ava didn't want the No Brides Club members picking that up from Kate.

Kate hugged her before hailing a cab to the Amtrak Station. "Remember I'm not far away if you need me."

"Yep." *Only two-and-a-half hours north.*

When the cab door closed behind Kate, Ava turned and walked the short distance to her apartment complex enjoying the warm, but not humid evening air and the buzz of the city. Her sister certainly was right. New York wasn't their two-convenience store/gas stations, one pizzeria, one family restaurant, and a hardware store hometown of Genesee.

Ava's phone chimed in the elevator on her way up to her floor. Kate checking on her already? Since the elevator was opening for her floor, she waited until she was in the apartment to look at the text. It was one of the temp agencies. She pressed the link for the assignment, fingers crossed that it was at a law firm. Tomorrow was probably the last full day she'd have to work since her law-prep program at NYU was starting Monday.

She uncrossed her fingers. It was a daycare sub.

At the athletic club here, again all day. Her two drinks took her to Nick Jansen's face again and the play of expressions that had crossed it when she and the twins had barged into his office. She was tempted to close the agency's app along with her unwanted visual response to seeing the Jansen Athletic Club name. But, even if she didn't have to pay rent on the apartment, she had other expenses, and could use the money. Turning the work down for some unfathomable aversion to seeing Nick Jansen again was ridiculous.

He probably had Mia and Lucas back with their mother, so she wouldn't be seeing him at the Kiddie Korner in the athletic club. And this was New York with 8.5 million people. Not Genesee with its 2,400 people. Chances were, she wouldn't run into Nick anywhere else again either.

———

*N*ick got the kids herded from the athletic club to the apartment he was subleasing while he was working for his uncle. At least that's what it felt like—herding. Mia and Lucas were five. Everything they saw was interesting. A note from the building super on the apartment door greeted them. The super didn't believe in texts or emails.

"What does it say, Uncle Nick? We can't read yet," Mia said.

"Is it from Mommy?" Lucas asked.

"No, it's from the building supervisor." Nick did a quick study of the twins' faces, Lucas's especially. He wasn't looking forward to any meltdowns this evening. They just looked curious. "He wants us to come and get your stuff."

"I'm hungry," Mia complained.

Nick checked his phone. It was going on seven. Waiting to feed them could trigger a meltdown. But he wouldn't blame them. They'd had quite a day. "I'll call the super and tell him we'll get your things after we eat." He unlocked the apartment door and followed the kids in.

They immediately checked out all the rooms, all two of them, a combination living room-kitchen with a bar divider and his bedroom. Three if you included the bath.

"Your house is pretty small," Mia declared.

It was, compared to the two-bedroom, bath-and-a-half condo with a formal dining room Constance had in Philadelphia that they'd shared during their engagement. And the twins had never been to the historic house he'd bought outside Philadelphia in Elwyn, near Media, PA, as an investment after Constance had broken their engagement. She'd thought a clean break would be best. Until now. He checked his email on his phone. No response from the email he'd sent her.

"I'm only one person and only here in New York while I'm helping my uncle at the athletic club. I have a house near Philadelphia." He rubbed the back of his neck. He didn't need to justify his living situation to them.

"Where are we going to sleep?" Lucas asked.

"Let's eat first and we can figure that out after we get your things." Seeing what Constance had had them bring might give him a clue of how long she planned for them to stay here.

"What do you have to eat?" Mia asked.

"I like SpaghettiOs," Lucas said.

"I remember. But, sorry bud, I don't have any." Nick opened the refrigerator and surveyed its contents: pizza, left over from last night—what he'd planned on having tonight—a plastic box of salad greens, bread, butter, a couple of apple ales, bottled water, and some grapes. He pulled out the pizza box. "How about pizza?"

"Does it have the pep … pep … circles on the top?" Mia asked.

"Yes, but I can take them off your piece if you want."

"No I like them."

Nick resisted checking his email again for something from Constance. He needed to get the twins fed and their stuff up here.

"Good. We'll have pizza and salad with grapes for dessert. Do you want orange juice to drink?" He had some concentrate in the freezer.

"I do," Mia said.

"Me, too, but you should put extra water in," Lucas said. "I seed on TV that straight orange juice is bad for you like soda."

Leave it to Mr. Details. "I'll add extra water."

Dinner went well enough. The kids must have been as hungry as they'd said. They'd eaten everything he'd given them. Nick put their plates and juice glasses in the sink for later. He'd nixed the ale he really would have liked until later when he had Mia and Lucas in bed. He called the super to tell him they were on their way.

"Come on, we need to get your things. Lucas, you can push the elevator button on the way down, and Mia, you can push it on the way up."

The superintendent met them at the building's temporary storage area in the basement and unlocked the gate.

"How much of this is theirs?" Nick waved toward the twins.

"All of it," the super answered.

Nick stared into the fenced area. Two giant suitcases, two pull along suitcases, two crates. "The crates, too?"

"Yep," the super said.

"Must be everything they own," Nick muttered.

"No," Mia said. "Not our bicycles. Mommy said we wouldn't have any place to ride them."

"You're going to need the package cart," the super said.

He was going to need something, *or he'd have to make four trips.*

Nick moved the suitcases and crates out of the storage area while the superintendent got the cart, which looked like a utility version of a hotel luggage cart. His hands slipped and he dropped the second crate with a loud thud. "What have you got in these?"

"Our toys," Mia said.

"Wait until you see all my cars and trucks," Lucas piped up.

Nick and the super loaded the cart, and the super locked the storage area behind them.

"Go ahead and use the freight elevator," the super said.

Nick set Mia to holding the right side of the cart's handle and Lucas to the left and maneuvered the cart into the elevator. The door opened on their floor. "You two go ahead first and wait for me. Once you're out of the elevator, don't move."

The kids exited and stood to one side.

When Nick had the cart halfway out, Lucas said, "Look, there's Ms. Ava."

"I said, 'Don't move.'" Nick had anticipated their next action. Mia's at least: running after some strange woman.

Nick pushed the cart the rest of the way out and looked over the luggage to see a slim dark-haired figure in a black and white dress disappearing into one of the apartments. One of the many higher-level professionals who lived in the building. The type of women he was attracted to when he had the time for the luxury of dating.

"I don't think that was Ms. Ava." She struck him as more of an apartment-across-the-river-in-New Jersey-with-four-roommates-type. Not that he'd had any problem with that type of woman when he was younger, when he'd needed a diversion from his grueling schedule of sixty-hour workweeks in the mergers and acquisitions unit of the communications giant he'd worked for in Philadelphia and every other weekend of intensive classes at Wharton.

But, now, at thirty, he had more of an eye for a professional equal who understood the need to balance dedication to work with a personal life, as he did now. Women who were interested in short-term companionship, which was all he had in him to offer.

3

"**Ms. Ava!**" Mia and Lucas raced into the Kiddie Korner the next morning with a woman sporting a look of displeasure.

Their mother? Ava could imagine what Nick might have said when he'd reached her.

"Hi, guys," Ava said.

"Ms. Lewis, I'm Maggie O'Shay, the center's manager."

So not the twins' mother.

"As you may or may not know, the Kiddie Korner is strictly drop-in childcare for our members while using the facility."

"I'm only a temp employee, but I'm aware." Not that it mattered much, since today would probably be her last day. She wouldn't be taking any temp assignments while attending her summer program. At least not any childcare ones. She couldn't say she wouldn't try to juggle one in a law office to add to her resume.

"Yes. Well, you're going to have Mr. Jansen's, Nick Jansen's," she clarified, "niece and nephew all day today. I didn't want you to be concerned about rules being broken. Because he's here working for our corporate owner Peter Jansen, I'm allowing the children to stay in the Kiddie Korner full time for a short period until other arrangements can be made."

Ava generally had no tolerance for people who used who they knew to take advantage, but she had sympathy for the spot Nick was in.

"Here are the children's registration forms," the manager said.

Ava took the forms to put in the file cabinet with the incomplete ones from yesterday.

"And Mr. Jansen said to tell you they have lunches in their backpacks. I thought it was better for me, rather than their uncle to bring the children this morning, so I could explain the situation."

"Thank, you," Ava said.

The manager left and the children glued themselves to her, one on either side.

"When we said our bedtime prayers last night with Uncle Nick, we prayed that you would be here today," Mia said.

Lucas nodded. "He said not to count on it."

"But here I am."

"You're funny, Ms. Ava," Lucas said.

"Let's get your backpacks off and lunches in the refrigerator."

The kids wrestled out of their packs and duly handed her two brown bags.

"We don't have lunch boxes," Mia said almost apologetically. "At Pre-K, we got lunches."

"We had to take our lunches to day camp," Lucas said.

"That was last year," Mia added.

"Yeah," Lucas said with a sigh of patience far beyond his years. "Mommy didn't sign us up this year because they said Mia was corrugated or something."

"Incorrigible?" Ava slapped her hand over her mouth, but the word had already escaped.

"That's it," he said.

"They only said that because I pushed a girl off the dock who couldn't swim. How did I know she couldn't swim?" Mia asked.

Lucas looked around the playroom. "Are we the only ones here?"

"For now," Ava answered. "More kids may come later. What would you guys like to do?"

Lucas's eyes lit when he saw the puzzles in the bookcase. "Let's do a puzzle, Mia." He raced over. "They have one with trucks."

"I want to go outside," Mia said. "Is there a playground?"

"No, but we may be able to go play in the gym a little later, after we see if anyone else is coming this morning."

"Oh-kay. I'll do a puzzle with Lucas." Mia dropped to the rug by the bookcase with a heavy sigh.

Ava studied the two blond heads bent over the puzzle. Although Nick's hair was darker with more red in it, the children had enough of the same coloring as he did to be his actual niece and nephew. Her first impression of disgust where he'd reminded her of her ex had faded. She saw past the superficial, which was a whole new issue.

The arrival of Louisa and several other children pushed Nick out of her mind, where she hoped he stayed. She had too much at stake to be detoured by a relationship right now.

"Anyone here up to joining me for lunch?" Nick asked from the doorway of the small gym several hours later. The contrast of his deep voice over the children's startled Ava.

She looked over her shoulder at him from the Nerf dodgeball game she was trying to keep going with Lucas and Mia—unsuccessfully, now that the other kids had been retrieved by their parents. She'd been enjoying the kids so much that she didn't know where the time had gone.

"Uncle Nick." Mia skipped over and grabbed his hand. "Come and play."

Part of Ava's plan of pushing lunch off and keeping the game going had been to take the edge off Mia's boundless energy so she could sit still for the *Bob the Builder* DVD Lucas had asked if they could watch after lunch.

Nick strode over with Mia. "Sorry, pumpkin, I don't have a long enough lunch break to play."

From what Ava had gathered from Louisa this morning, Nick was a private business consultant and his own boss. Granted, the aide had said Nick's business was still a startup, but couldn't he take a long lunch break if he wanted? She studied the cleft in

Nick's chin, not meeting his eyes. That competition for time. That's why she wanted to be established and successful in her law career before she tackled any romantic relationship or thoughts of her own kids, as much as she liked kids.

"I thought we could take our lunches outside to the courtyard and have a picnic," Nick said.

"I told Ms. Ava I wanted to go outside before," Mia complained.

Nick's gaze met Ava's for the first time since he'd arrived. She blinked. His hazel eyes had flecks of blue that she hadn't noticed before.

Ava broke the contact. Okay, so he had intriguing eyes. So what? She should be ... *was* ... more affected by how needy Mia and Lucas were, each in their own way.

Maybe she should talk with Nick when he picked up the kids after work, except what authority would she be speaking from? All she had was a bachelor's degree in early childhood education. That authority would come in time from her dual law and masters in social work degrees.

"Come on, Mia, you know you can't always get what you want," Nick said.

The little girl shrugged. "But it's worth a try."

Nick's laughter, rich and warm like a premium

hot chocolate, soothed Ava's jumbled thoughts and concerns about Mia and Lucas.

"As long as you don't push back too hard," Nick said.

"I don't know what you mean," Mia said.

The smug look on her face told Ava that Mia had a pretty good understanding of what Nick had said. Ava caught a slight tensing of his facial muscles before they relaxed into a neutral expression. She doubted she could tell Nick anything about the twins that he didn't already know. Besides, it wasn't her business.

When they reached the Kiddie Korner and she opened the door, Lucas dashed in ahead of everyone else, more in the mode of his sister than what Ava had seen so far with him. Seconds later he marched out of the kitchenette holding a brown bag in each hand.

"I got our lunches." He said with a big smile on his face. "I didn't find one for you, Ms. Ava."

"Lucas." Mia jammed her hands onto her hips. "Ms. Ava said we weren't 'sposed to go in the kitchen room."

"I was just trying to help."

"It's okay this time." Ava's phone buzzed in her pocket. She pulled it out and checked the caller ID.

It was the Howland Scholarship Fund. "You guys go ahead. I'll join you in a minute." She pressed the "accept call" button and walked to the kitchenette to get her lunch salad.

"Ms. Lewis. This is the Howland Scholarship Fund. We have your scholarship application for the fall semester, but we're missing your elementary school records verifying that you were in Miss Howland's kindergarten class. The deadline to have your records to us for the Fall is Monday."

Ava's throat constricted. She was counting on this scholarship—it had been created by her kindergarten teacher to help her former students with full college tuition for any four years of college classes. The Genesee Central school office was only open a couple days a week in the summer. Her mind raced with ways she could get the information to the scholarship fund in time until she hit on one. She cleared her throat. "I used the first year of my available scholarship three years ago for my freshman year at Genesee Community College. Would you still have my records from then on file?"

"We should. Let me check." the voice on the other side of the call said.

Ava tapped her fingers on the countertop while she waited.

"Yes, we do have those records. You're all set."

"Thanks." Ava's knees went weak with relief as the caller hung up. She couldn't afford to lose the scholarship. She got her lunch out of the refrigerator and headed back to the playroom.

"You waited for me," she said when she saw that Nick and the kids were still there.

"Yeah. I've got this. Lunch. You look like you need a break."

Ava pushed her bangs back. Did she really look that ragged? "Thanks. I wouldn't mind one."

He shuffled the twins out the door to protests of "Isn't Ms. Ava coming?"

She dropped onto the couch and opened her salad container. Nick was right. She could use a break. And the professional code for teachers—even part-time, temporary childcare teachers—discouraged them from socializing with their students' parents or guardians. Not to mention her No Brides Club vow to forgo male distractions until she reached her professional goal. So what was with the disappointment flooding her that the kids were having lunch with Nick, and she wasn't?

———

Nick arrived at the Kiddie Korner to pick up the kids with ten minutes to spare until it closed for dinner hour, only to find that Ava had already left. No big deal, except for the nagging need he had to show her he was a responsible person where Mia and Lucas were concerned. Or was it to show himself that he'd moved beyond total focus on his career?

"You guys ready to go?" he asked.

"Yes, we put all our stuff in our backpacks," Mia said.

"By ourselves," Lucas added.

"Then, let's go." Nick opened the door and shot a "thanks" over to the woman staffing the room.

"We're going out for hamburgers," he said as they walked the short hall to the apartment complex's main door.

"French fries, too?" Mia asked, skipping right beside him for a change.

"French fries, too."

"Can I have a cheeseburger?" Lucas asked.

"Certainly."

An elevator opened beside them, and people filed out.

"Ms. Ava," Lucas shouted.

Ava stopped and turned toward them.

"See Uncle Nick. I told you Ms. Ava lived here," Mia said. "We're going to get hamburgers. What are you doing?"

"Mia, manners," Nick said. "That's not really our business." But the little girl had him curious now.

Ava laughed, her eye crinkling slightly at the corners. Maybe she wasn't as young as he'd thought. Or she might be a person who laughed a lot.

"It's okay. I'm going out to eat, too. Celebrating my law-prep classes starting on Monday."

A law student. She was as young as he'd originally thought—not that that should mean anything to him.

"You still go to school?" Lucas asked wide-eyed.

"We went to the Pre-K class and after the summer's over, we're going to kindergarten," Mia shared.

"I used to teach Pre-K."

"Then, why are you going to school?" Lucas scrunched his face as if he was thinking that question over really hard.

"I want to become a lawyer who helps children."

"Oh." Lucas didn't look satisfied with that answer but didn't say anymore.

Nick looked from Lucas to Ava. Not only was the

woman young, but naïve. He cleared his throat. "You might not want to be sharing your life history with a man you don't know."

"Yes, you shouldn't talk to strangers," Mia backed him up.

Secure in his warning, Nick waited for a protest from Ava. He was only protecting her.

Instead, Ava slapped her hand to her lips and laughed. "You're absolutely right. My country roots are showing. I'm from a small place in Western New York, where I know just about everyone."

"New York City is different."

"I know." Ava's voice was less cordial.

"But where's the stranger?" Lucas asked.

Nick and Ava laughed together, gaining the group dirty looks from some of the people exiting the elevators.

"We're blocking people. I should get going," Ava said.

"Enjoy your celebration." Ava was probably meeting friends. Maybe a boyfriend. A beautiful young woman like her would have no lack of male attention. All the more reason to heed his own warning.

Nick took Lucas's hand and reached for Mia's, coming up empty. He sighed and scanned the area around the elevators. Mia loved riding elevators. His chest tightened. She wouldn't have …

"Can I pet the dog, too?" Lucas asked.

"What dog?"

"The one Mia's petting." He pointed to the bank of mailboxes on the side wall, where Mia squatted petting a small dog on a leash while an elderly woman smiled down at her.

In three strides that had little Lucas trotting, Nick was beside Mia and the woman.

Over her shoulder, Mia said, "I didn't talk to the strange lady. Only to the dog."

The woman laughed. "You have your hands full with that one."

"Indeed, I do."

"Can I pet the dog?" Lucas asked again.

"You may," the woman said.

Lucas patted the dog's head.

"Come on," Nick said. "I don't know about you, but I'm hungry."

"Bye," the woman said.

Nick nodded at the dog and the kids. "Bye and thanks." He took the twins firmly by the hands and walked them to a small family style restaurant known for its burgers.

"Look, there's Ms. Ava," Mia said when he opened the restaurant's door. And off she went.

He should have let go of Lucas's hand to open the door, rather than Mia's. Nick walked Lucas to the hostess station where Ava stood to one side with several other people. The others were older. Didn't look like they'd be Ava's friends. But what did he know?

"Hi," Ava said. "Mia invited me to join you. I have a long wait for a small table, so I took one for four that the bus person is clearing now. Uh, I hope you don't mind. That is—mind me joining you."

"Not at all." Nick took in the white tank top tucked into her navy shorts and the way it emphasized the flare of her hips, while he subdued the smile that had threatened to erupt in response to her refreshing lack of guile. *Why would I mind eating with a beautiful woman?*

Nick swallowed and raised his gaze to her face. Had he said that out loud?

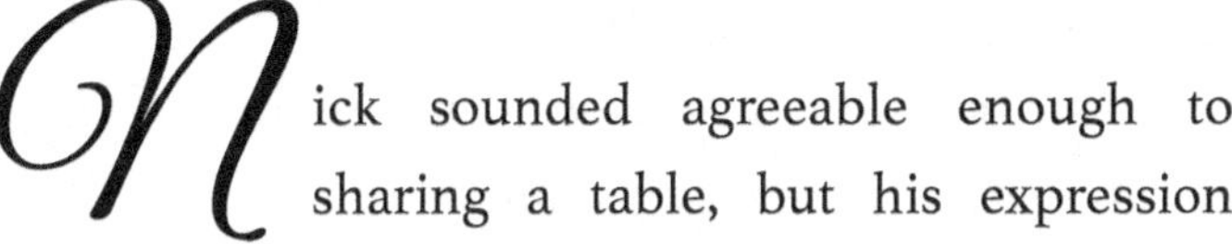

*N*ick sounded agreeable enough to sharing a table, but his expression looked as if he had a mouthful of Sour Patch Kids candies. He could have said no.

"Party of four?"

The hostess interrupted Ava's thoughts.

"This way, please." The hostess led them to a table in the back and passed out menus. She had throwaway color-in ones for the kids, along with crayons. "Your server will be with you shortly."

Ava picked up her menu, while Nick helped the twins with their choices.

"I thought you might be celebrating with friends," Nick said out of the blue.

She jerked her head up from the menu. She'd only moved to New York two weeks ago. She didn't have any friends to celebrate with, except the women she'd met at the No Brides Club meeting yesterday. Nick's earlier warning about telling strange men her life story popped into her head. "I celebrated with them last night. Tonight, I just felt like a burger, and heard good things about this place." No need to tell *him* the good things had been on a TV commercial.

"You won't be disappointed. They make great burgers and desserts. I haven't tried anything else."

A server approached their table. "Hi, I'm Will,

your server tonight. Are you ready to order or do you need more time?"

Nick looked at her, and she nodded. "Ladies first," he said.

"I'll have a double bacon cheeseburger platter and plain iced tea."

Will jotted on his pad. "And would you like melted cheddar on your fries?"

"Why not?" Hey, she'd had a salad for lunch. She handed her menu to the server.

"Mia, you're next," Nick prompted.

"Do you have hotdogs?"

Nick laughed. "Leave it to Mia to want a hotdog at a burger joint."

"Yes, we have hotdogs," Will said.

"I want a hotdog, fries, and milk. Chocolate milk."

"I want chocolate milk, too," Lucas said. "And what Ms. Ava is having. A cheeseburger and fries but no cheddar stuff."

"Okay, so we have a children's hotdog meal and a children's cheeseburger meal."

"Right." Nick confirmed, and as he placed his order, the twin's launched into a game of twenty questions with Ava.

"Do you have brothers and sisters?" Mia asked.

"I do, a sister and a brother."

"Are you bigger than them?" Lucas joined in.

"They're both older than I am."

"Do they boss you around?"

Ava smiled at Lucas. "Sometimes."

"I'm Mia's big brother,"

"By 17 minutes is all," Mia said

Lucas's shoulders slumped. "Mia bosses me around all the time, anyway. "I wish we had a younger brother or sister."

"Me, too," Mia said. "But Mommy's boyfriend doesn't like kids."

"Carson isn't her boyfriend anymore. They got married." Lucas corrected. "That's what Mommy's note and Nana said, right?" He tilted his head up at Nick.

"You got in contact with their mother, then?" Ava said. She extinguished the pang that she'd miss them when they left. She had no expectations of seeing them again. Once she started her summer program, she'd be too busy and have no reason to see them, even if they continued to stay with Nick. It wasn't as if she would be taking any more temp childcare work at the athletic club.

"I got a hold of their grandmother," Nick explained.

"Mommy's on her honeymoon. We were supposed to stay with Mrs. Harris, but she had to take a vacation. Mrs. Harris is our housekeeper." Lucas filled her in.

"Guys, why don't you color your pictures? For Ms. Ava." Nick's words sounded like they were strained through his gritted teeth.

"Okay," the twins said, and the table fell quiet.

The server returned with their drinks. Ava accepted hers and sipped the tea until she couldn't stand it any longer. "So, you talked with the twins' grandmother. Will she be coming for the twins, or will you be taking them back to the Philadelphia area? I assume they live there, too."

Nick stared at her.

"I Googled you and saw your business is based in Philadelphia."

Nick arched an eyebrow and she shivered.

"L-last night," she stuttered. "I thought about the twins and my leaving them with you. I felt I should check." Even though he was listed as a contact on the incomplete registration form from the twins' mother. "Isn't that what everyone does when they meet someone new?"

His expression turned smug, as if despite her

emphasis on Mia and Lucas, she'd checked him out because she was interested in him.

Yeah, right. The only thing she could allow herself to be interested in was law school and establishing her law career. "You didn't answer my question."

"It looks like I'll have Mia and Lucas for a few weeks. Their mother is on a month-long cruise with her new husband. Her mother's schedule is too full to take the twins, and Mrs. Harris, Constance's housekeeper, quit. I think, rather than take on the kids for a month."

"They can't be that bad," Ava said.

"No, they're not. But Constance hired Mrs. Harris as a housekeeper, not a nanny, and the month-long 24-7 was probably more than she could, or wanted to, handle. I can't take a month off work. So it looks like I'm going to have to find someone to help watch them until Constance gets back. Any recommendations?"

Ava shook her head before thinking. "Wait, maybe. You could start with the temp agency that the athletic club uses to get people to fill in at the Kiddie Korner. And I have the names of two other agencies I signed with.

Uncertainty clouded his face. "I'd want the same person for however long I have them."

"Of course. The work assignment can be as long or short as you want, even open-ended."

"Let's hope it doesn't come to that. They shouldn't be subjected to that instability."

Ava agreed. "I'll give you my cards. I have the agency apps, so I don't need them back." And she wasn't planning on taking any more childcare gigs. "Here." She slid the business cards across the table to him.

"You're talking about us, aren't you?" Mia said.

Ava gulped. She'd thought the kids had been too involved in their coloring to listen in on her and Nick's conversation. Not brilliant on her part. "Yes. You guys will need someone to stay with you while your uncle works."

"We can come to work with Uncle Nick and stay with you," Lucas said.

"I won't be at the athletic club anymore." Ava said. "I'm starting school. Remember?"

Lucas's lips turned down and his forehead wrinkled.

"Look," Nick said with forced joviality. "Our food is here."

The action of the server placing their dinners on

the table gave Ava time to regroup. Lucas looked like he was going to have a meltdown.

"Wait. I know." Lucas's eyes brightened. "We can go to school with you. At Pre-K, one of the teachers brought her little boy with her. He was five like us."

"Sorry, I can't."

"Why not?" Mia demanded. "I thought you liked us."

"Yeah," Lucas said.

Ava's throat clogged, her heart squeezing with thoughts of what the twins were probably feeling. Those thoughts quickly moved on to ways she might work around school to help care for the twins.

"Lucas, Mia." Nick's voice cut in. "Eat your food and let Ms. Ava eat hers."

"But Uncle Nick," they whined.

"No, buts. Eat."

Ava picked up her fork and cleared her thoughts. She wasn't a teacher or a childcare worker anymore. She was a law student and a member of the No Brides Club. She'd taken a vow to not let anything interfere with her career goals. Ava looked up from her plate to the twins glaring at Nick. Or Anyone. Not even adorable little people like Mia and Lucas .... Or their gorgeous uncle.

Nick attacked his food as if it was trying to get

away, and the kids were unusually quiet while they ate. Ava picked at her plate and finally gave in and flagged their server for her check and a take-out box.

An older woman stopped by the table at the same time the server brought her box and check. Mia and Lucas perked up and asked the woman about her dog. Ava grabbed her food and check, mumbling something to Nick about having to get home, and waved goodbye to the kids before making a beeline to the cash-out counter and the front door.

Outside, the air was as thick and charged as the air around their table had been. She dragged herself home and dropped onto the couch, congratulating herself for her exit from Nick and the twins.

This time, a year ago, she would have been sucked in. Jumped at lending Nick a hand and watching Mia and Lucas for the summer, instead of what she felt now—defensive that he might even ask her for help finding someone to care for the twins. But last year, she'd been engaged to Trey, starry-eyed and thinking of their future kids. Lost in her own world of happily ever after.

Now she'd been dosed with realism. She couldn't let her heart and emotions make her decisions. She had to make them with her head. She had to show her parents, Kate, her brother Josh, and herself that she wasn't the flighty, girlie-girl that people thought she was. She was a strong woman who could stand on her own two feet. A woman who was as smart as her siblings and would someday be as financially successful as well.

However, at the moment, she felt like a wrung-out washcloth; worried about what was going to happen with Mia and Lucas and sympathetic to Nick and his childcare dilemma. Ava pressed her fingertips to her temples, glad to be back at her place alone. Tomorrow she'd take on her mantle of iron again.

4

These are my people, Ava thought as she left the lecture hall on the NYU campus Monday afternoon. People like the No Brides Club members who were on their way to career success. For the most part, it was exactly what she'd expected. What she hadn't expected was that she'd be drawn to the older students at lunch and when they broke up into discussion groups, to students who were pursuing law after working at something else. The students she'd met who were fresh from earning their bachelor's degree and more her age, seemed so young.

"See you tomorrow," one of the guys from her discussion group called as she turned in the direction of her apartment complex.

"Right. Bright and early." That was another thing she hadn't expected. The law-prep program enrollment was so large that the law school dean had divided the group into two sections, one meeting from 7:00 am to 1:00 pm and the other meeting from 1:00 pm to 7:00 pm, starting tomorrow. Normally, the program ran 9:00 to 4:00 with an hour for lunch. She'd lucked out and gotten the early section, leaving her free to try to pick up some afternoon law office temp assignments. She'd still have evenings free for her class work.

She stopped by the mailboxes in the building lobby and saw the older woman who'd stopped to talk with Nick at the restaurant Friday. "Hi," Ava said.

The woman closed her mailbox and turned her head toward Ava. "Hello. I'm Ellen Murphy. I didn't get a chance to introduce myself at the restaurant. You left so quickly."

Ava flushed. She had been a little rude. More than a little. "Ava Lewis." She opened her mailbox and removed the contents. *Junk mail.*

"Your friend Nick certainly has his job cut for him out with those twins, especially Mia," Ellen said.

Friend? Were she and Nick friends? No, more

like acquaintances. "He sure does have his work cut out for him." More than Ellen probably knew.

"It was nice seeing you again," Ellen said

"Yes, nice meeting you."

Ellen's heals clicked on the tile floor as she walked away, and Ava's thoughts went to Nick and the kids. And her free afternoons. *Darn.* She wished Ellen hadn't mentioned them. She'd prided herself on having been able to almost completely block them out of her mind for the weekend. *Some of the time.*

Ava stepped out of the elevator and caught a flash of color on the floor down the hall toward her apartment. She turned in that direction. It was ... she blinked to make sure. It was Lucas sitting on the floor. She rushed to him.

"Hi, Ms. Ava." He stood.

"Lucas, what are you doing here. Where are Mia and your uncle?"

"Mia went to the bathroom with the lady."

Ava's throat closed.

"And Uncle Nick is at a meeting."

Working to keep the panic out of her voice, Ava asked, "Mia went with what lady? Show me where."

"The lady who got us from your Kiddie Korner when Mia got us throwed out."

Ava took the little boy's hand. It wasn't *her* Kiddie Korner. Not that that mattered. "Show me where the lady took Mia?" she repeated, dragging him behind her to the elevator and punching the L button as the elevator door closed.

"Uncle Nick lets me and Mia take turns pushing the buttons."

"Sorry. I'm in a hurry. We have to find Mia."

"I know where she is. She went to the bathroom with the lady."

Lucas's certainty did not reassure Ava at all. The elevator dinged and flashed a stop at another floor. "How did you get up to my apartment?" she asked so she wouldn't scream at the elevator to not make any more stops.

"I pushed 22 and when I got off, I counted doors from Uncle Nick's door. I wasn't sure if it was ten or eleven so I sat in the middle."

Ava didn't even want to ask how Lucas knew how many doors her apartment was from Nick's.

Finally, the elevator opened onto the lobby. Ava whisked Lucas out, heart racing. "Show me where you last saw Mia."

Lucas cocked his head as if he didn't understand, then he led her to the office where Nick had been working the other day.

She pushed open the door.

"That's the lady," Lucas said.

Maggie, the athletic club's manager, who'd brought the kids to the Kiddie Korner on Friday spun around, setting her phone on the desk beside her. "Lucas, where have you been," she screeched. "I've been looking all over for you."

Lucas cowered, and Ava put her arm around his shoulder. Before she could say anything, Lucas spoke.

"I didn't like being in your room by myself. You tooked so long, I went to Uncle Nick's `partment and knocked. He wasn't there," Lucas said in a soft voice.

Maggie turned on Ava. Her eyes narrowed.

Probably recognizing her as the temp from the Kiddie Korner.

"Did you take him there?" Maggie asked.

"I did not. I found Lucas sitting in the hall on the 22nd floor, where my apartment is."

"Uncle Nick's too," Mia chimed in.

"Yep, I counted the doors to Ms. Ava's," Lukas said.

Ava smiled the validation she knew Lucas craved.

"You know where Ms. Ava lives?" Mia asked.

"Yep. `member when we saw Ms. Ava in the hall,

and Uncle Nick said it wasn't her? It was Ms. Ava."

"Cool!" Mia said.

Ava glanced around the office and saw the twins' backpacks emptied all around the room. "Lucas and Mia, please pick up your things and put them in your backpacks. I need to talk with Ms. O'Shay."

"Okay," Mia said. "Can we have a race to see who gets done first?"

"Sure." She didn't have a lot to say to the manager. Ava faced Maggie. "You left a five-year-old alone in a strange place?"

Maggie huffed. "Mia needed to go to the ladies' room. It would have been better to send her alone and stay with Lucas?"

Was the woman serious. "You had other choices. You could have checked the ladies' room to see if it was empty and taken both children in or stood just outside the room with Lucas while Mia went in."

Maggie shrugged. "I'm not a babysitter," she said as if that were somehow beneath her.

Ava rerouted her anger to sarcasm. "No, you're the club manager, which is far more important than the welfare of a child."

Maggie scoffed and opened her mouth to say something but was interrupted by Nick bursting into the office.

"Have you found Lucas? Louisa at the Kiddie Korner said you lost him, asked them to let you know if he came back there. Why aren't you out looking for him?" Nick stopped when he noticed Ava.

"Lucas is fine." Ava stepped aside so he could see the children putting their things in their backpacks. "When I got home from class, he was sitting outside my apartment door."

"What? How?"

"Maggie left him alone here in the office—"

"To take his sister to the ladies' room," Maggie interrupted.

"You left a five-year-old alone in a strange place?" Nick demanded.

"I told him to stay in my office. I'm not some kind of babysitter," Maggie repeated the excuse she'd given Ava.

"No, you're not responsible enough to be. Makes me wonder whether you're responsible enough to run the club," he said

Maggie snapped her mouth closed.

"Are you done yelling at the lady?" Mia asked as she and her brother joined them. "I finished first, Ms. Ava, right?"

"Only because she kicked my blue crayon under

the bookcase."

Nick draped his arm around Lucas. "You're okay, buddy?"

"Yep. I waited for Ms. Ava to come home."

"It's a good thing she found you there. I'll talk to you *and* your sister when we get home." Nick turned to Ava. "But how did he get up to your apartment?"

"Kids are smarter and more observant than adults give them credit for," she said.

"It was easy, Uncle Nick. I know how to use the elevator."

"How did you know which apartment was Ms. Ava's?"

"'member when we saw Ms. Ava? When we got our stuff from the guy? You said it wasn't Ms. Ava. I counted doors."

"I think I've got that. Thanks for your help, Ava. When I got out of my meeting and listened to Maggie's voicemail ..."

"No problem. I can imagine what you felt, and I won't tell you what I felt when Lucas said he'd been left alone." She shifted her weight from foot to foot. "Now, that you have things under control, I should be going."

His mumbled "As much as I can," brought a smile to her lips.

"See you around," she said.

"Bye. And thanks again."

"Bye Ms. Ava," the twins said.

"Bye." As Ava reached for the door handle, she heard Nick say, "Okay, guys, we're leaving too, as soon as I get some stuff from my desk to work at home tomorrow."

"With us?" Lucas asked. "Mia got us throwed out of daycare."

"Yes," Nick answered. "And we'll talk about that when we get upstairs."

Ava slipped through the door and let it close with a soft click. She thought of Ellen Murphy's word less than an hour before, Nick certainly did have his work cut out for him.

———

"**A**re you done yet?" Mia asked Nick for at least the fifth time. "We're bored. You said we could go to the park."

He had said that. A few hours ago when he'd given them breakfast. When he'd still had the illusion that he could concentrate on work with them there. He'd been at it for seven hours, minus time for lunch, and the only real progress he'd made was in the two hours before they'd gotten up and the hour he'd found a children's program for them to watch on TV.

"I'm done for now." *More like done in.* When the twins had been playing noisily, he'd keep looking up and checking on them, breaking his concentration on his work. When they, especially Mia, were too quiet or out of sight, he couldn't work for wondering what they were up to.

"I'm all ready," Mia announced.

"Can you help me? There's a knot in my sneaker," Lucas said.

"Sure thing. While I help Lucas, Mia can you get my black shoes? They're by the bed."

"The ones with the panther on them?" she asked.

"A puma," he corrected. "But, yes. Those."

She raced out of the room, and had Nick wondering if he shouldn't have gotten his cross-trainers himself. He untangled Lucas's shoelace and went to see what was keeping Mia. She stood shoe-less with his shoes on her hands and was clapping them together.

"May I have my shoes?"

She pushed her hands forward, and he lifted them off her hands. He sat on the edge of the bed and put them on. "What were you doing?"

"I wanted to see if bigger shoes made a bigger noise. They do."

"Okay, with that determined, let's get our shoes on so we can go to the park." He could only hope that a trip to Washington Market Park would wear them out some so they might nap. And he could get some work done.

The building lobby was free of any distractions, so he and the twins made it directly to the exit door. But not through it.

"There's Ms. Ava." Lucas pointed out the glass door to the walkway to the building.

Nick frowned. She should be at her class. He pulled open the door. What was he doing? Ava was a grown woman. She could choose to ditch her afternoon class session if she wanted. But for some reason, that disappointed him.

"Hi, Ms. Ava," Mia said. "We're going to play on the swings."

"Is your school done?" Lucas asked. "Can you come with us?"

"Yes, and that's up to your uncle."

Nick tensed. *Just like Constance.* Ava was lying to appease the twins and asking him to back her. "I thought your classes were all day," he blurted.

"No, only until one. There are so many of us that

they split the group into two sessions. I took the seven to one to leave my afternoons free to temp if I get any offers."

Nick absorbed that information. Ava seemed to be free this afternoon. His thoughts raced ahead. Every afternoon. He reined his thoughts back to this afternoon. "Any chance you could take Mia and Lucas to the park for me?"

Something flickered in her eyes and was gone.

"I'll pay you," he offered.

Ava laughed. "To take them off your hands?"

He grinned back. "Rough morning."

"I'd love to take Mia and Lucas to the park."

Was she stretching the truth now to flatter him? Constance had done that, too.

"Rethinking your offer?" Ava asked.

He shook his head to get his mind straight as much as to indicate he would like her to take the twins to the park.

"And you don't have to pay me. After this morning's taste of law school, it will be fun."

Her eyelids twitched again. At the exaggeration? It must be the stress of not getting any work done this morning. He was comparing Ava to Constance. Ava had been a preschool teacher. She probably wasn't exaggerating about taking the kids to the park being fun. From what he'd seen so far, Ava was nothing like Constance.

"Great. Thanks."

"Two things, first," Ava said.

He clenched his teeth. *Here it comes.*

"First, I need to run up and change my clothes."

Nick checked out her skirt and short-sleeved jacket and ran his gaze down her tanned legs to her closed-toe dress shoes.

Her gaze met his as he looked back up. He rubbed the back of his neck. He *had* started out just checking her clothes.

"I'm kind of over-dressed," she said.

"The kids and I can wait here for you." *And I can regroup.* "What's the second thing?"

"I need to know where the park is."

Nick gave her the address, which she put into her phone, and directions for how to get there. They also exchanged phone numbers.

"I'll be back in a few minutes," Ava said.

Nick watched her walk to the elevator.

"Isn't Ms. Ava coming to the park with us?" Lucas asked.

"Didn't you listen," Mia said before Nick could answer. "Ms. Ava is taking us."

"I was watching the cars," Lucas protested.

Nick squatted to their eye level. "I want you two to behave for Ms. Ava. No arguing with each other or Ms. Ava. Do what she says, or she may not take you again."

He didn't know why he'd said that. Except for a niggling idea in the back of his mind that he didn't want to give credence to.

"I will," they each said.

"Good." He rose.

"What about our ice cream?" Mia asked. "You always get us ice cream when you take us to the park."

Nick hadn't taken them to the park in Philadelphia more than a couple times and didn't recall any ice cream being involved, but that was the sort of thing Mia would have glommed onto if he had.

"I'll give Ms. Ava money for ice cream."

"Okay. For Ms. Ava, too?"

"For Ms. Ava, too, if she wants."

Mia and Lucas smiled up at him before being distracted by the flashing lights of a police car racing by.

The elevator dinged, and Nick looked over his shoulder to see if it was Ava already. A middle-aged man got off, and a pizza deliverer got on. The pizza made Nick wonder if Ava had had any lunch? She was just home from class. His gaze dropped to the twins, who had their noses practically pressed to the door glass. He needed a break from them more than he'd realized. Ava was a grown woman. He didn't need to be concerned about whether she'd eaten or anything else personal about her.

"All set." Ava's voice seemed to come out of nowhere.

He hadn't heard the elevator or her footsteps in the near-empty lobby. He mentally put coffee to break his fog at the top of his afternoon work schedule.

"Ms. Ava," Lucas said. "Uncle Nick said you can get us ice cream. All of us."

"Is that so," Ava said. "You like ice cream?"

"Yes," both children shouted, Mia jumping up and down.

"I also told them no arguing and to behave for you."

"Or else you wouldn't take us to the park again." Mia added.

Ava raised an eyebrow.

Nick concentrated on removing a bill from his wallet. "This should take care of ice cream for all of you." He handed Ava a couple of bills, keeping his wallet in his hand. "Did you have any lunch?"

He couldn't believe he said that.

"Not yet," she answered.

"Better give Ms. Ava more dollars for her lunch," Lucas said solemnly.

Ava ruffled the little boy's hair, while Nick fingered another $20 bill in his wallet.

"It's okay, *Uncle Nick*, I'll grab something from one of the street vendors near the park and have Mia and Lucas back by five."

He watched a grinning Ava leave with the twins. He'd deserved that. But having Ava see him as Uncle Nick was about the last thing he wanted—even though it was probably for the best. For both of them.

———

*A*va and the twins were skipping up Murray Street when she saw him. *Nick.* Striding toward them. It was after five, but not much. She stopped skipping and matched her walking stride to the kids' skipping. She didn't want Nick thinking she was irresponsible. Her stomach dropped. Or worse, have him see her as a child herself, as her family still too often did. He was older, but not that much older. She'd guess early thirties, like Kate and their brother

Josh. Not too old be friends, friendly neighbors. She missed her friends in Genesee, having people to hang with.

"Didn't you hear me?" Mia tugged on her hand.

Not hear Mia? But she hadn't.

"There's Uncle Nick," the little girl said.

As if Ava didn't know.

"I hope he wasn't coming to play with us at the park," Lucas said.

"No, I don't think so," Ava said.

"Hey," Nick said when they reached them. "I finished what I was working on and came to meet you."

"Whew!" Lucas said.

Ava silently agreed.

The little boy dropped her hand and wrapped his arms around Nick's legs. "I was `fraid you were coming to play with us at the park and would be sad we're done."

"Did you have fun?" Nick asked.

"Yes!" Lucas said.

"Sort of," Mia answered. "I tried to be friends with this girl, but she didn't want to."

Ava hadn't realized that. Her chest tightened. Sort of like she'd tried this morning at her class, but everyone had been too competitive to be social. She had a feeling she was going to really need the No Brides Club members to make her transition to life in the City.

"I'm sorry to hear that," Nick said. "Otherwise, did you have fun?"

"Yes, your playground has a curly slide," Mia said.

"You can't beat a curly slide," he said.

Ava mostly listened as the twins filled the walk back to the apartment complex with what they'd done at the park, what kind of ice cream they'd gotten, and what Ava had for lunch.

The group stopped at Nick's apartment.

"I'll see you guys," Ava said

"Bye, Ms. Ava," Mia said.

"When?" Lucas asked.

"Soon, I hope. I had fun with you at the park." That should be noncommittal enough to not mislead the twins, since she didn't know when or if.

Lucas grinned. "Me, too."

"Well, I should get these two in and fed." Nick didn't make any move to unlock the apartment door.

"Yes, I'm guessing these guys are hungry and t-i-r-e-d." Ava spelled out the last word.

"I don't know what that spells," Mia said.

"Nor do you need to," Nick answered.

The little girl huffed. "Grown-up stuff?"

"Yep," Nick said.

A quiet fell over the group. "You may be able to get some more work in," Ava said to fill it and ease her discomfort at Nick looking at her, but not saying anything.

"About that ... work ... Can I give you a call later when..." He tipped his head toward the kids. "If it's not too late."

"It shouldn't be. They played hard." Curiosity teased her. She had three ideas about what Nick wanted to talk with her about. Two solid ones and the third a wish she shouldn't be wishing.

"Okay, talk to you later." Nick unlocked the door.

"Later," she said, waiting until the door closed behind Nick and the twins before she walked up the hall to her apartment.

Ava made a sandwich for supper and went to work on her class assignment with as much of an eye on her laptop's clock as on the web assignment. But she still jumped when her phone rang at 9:00. It was Kate, not Nick.

She took a deep breath to slow her racing pulse and answered. "Hi."

"Hi, yourself. I wanted to check in on your first day of classes."

"It was great. Everyone seemed so focused on the lecture and the materials."

"Not like high school, huh?"

"Not at all. Nor, like community college." Since Ava had breezed through both with decent grades, little work, and lots of socializing, that was no over-statement.

"You know I, and the rest of the No Brides Club, are available to talk anytime you need to. We know what it's like being a woman in what, unfortunately, can still seem like a man's world."

"I know. I'm good so far." She had a quick thought about telling Kate about her loneliness but was interrupted by a beep on her phone. *Nick.* "Hey, I have another call I should take."

"That's our Ava, making friends already. Okay, I'll check back in with you later in the week."

"Talk to you then." Ava quickly ended the call and answered Nick's, holding her breath that it hadn't been sent to her voicemail already.

"Hello."

"Hi. Sorry, I'm calling later than I expected. Mia and Lucas got a second wind after I fed them, and I just got them to sleep. They're camping out in a blanket fort they made in my bedroom."

Ava laughed and then bit her tongue. "I shouldn't have laughed."

"No you shouldn't," he admonished her in a playful tone. "Do you know how long it took me to come up with the fort idea?" Nick didn't wait for her answer. "I have another idea I'd like to discuss with you. In person. Could you come over?"

Ava thought back to what she'd figured his idea most likely was. And if she was right, she should quell it right now. But a mental picture of the desperation on Nick's face when she ran into him after class today wouldn't let her.

"Okay. I'll be over in a minute."

Nick answered his door on the first knock and waved her in. "Sit down. Can I get you iced tea or water? An apple ale?"

"Iced tea is good." Ava settled into a recliner in the small living room.

"It's peach-herbal something. The twins like it."

"That's fine."

Nick walked around the counter divider that separated the kitchen from the living room and took out two bottles from the refrigerator—tea for her and ale for him—and opened them before placing the drinks on the coffee table and sitting on the couch.

He raked his hand through his hair. "I haven't been able to find openings for Mia and Lucas at any day camps in Manhattan. Nor did I have any success with the temp places you gave me."

Ava swallowed her mouthful of tea. The temp agency she'd worked through at the athletic club had sent her a childcare job over the weekend. When she'd seen "childcare," she declined it without reading the job details.

"So you'd like my help finding care for Mia and Lucas?"

"Your help, yes, but not exactly that."

Ava knew what was coming. "I have class every day Monday through Friday." She watched him rub his index finger up and down the sweat on the side of his ale bottle.

"But not in the afternoon." He shot her a killer smile.

She fortified her resistance. "I'll need time to do my assignments, to go to the law library on campus. That's not somewhere I'd take the twins."

Nick laughed, a deep full laugh, taking a chink out of her resistance. He sobered. "I'll lay it out. I should be able to do my work if you can take care of the kids Monday through Friday 1:30 to 6:30, and all day Saturday. I can do the rest when I have them in the morning and after they go to bed."

"That's a lot of hours."

"But it's only for four weeks, a day fewer than four weeks. It'll end before your class."

It wasn't as if she couldn't do it. She'd worked full time and carried a full academic load at Empire State College, the State University of New York's online, distance learning campus to finish her Bachelors of Education degree. But law school was supposed to be a break from her old life. And, it would leave her no time to pick up any law firm temp assignments. Not that she'd been able to so far, even with her entire day free.

Nick leaned toward her, arms parallel, elbows on knees. "I'd pay you a full-time wage." He mentioned a figure that made her eyes widen, almost twice what she'd earned as a Pre-K teacher in Genesee.

Granted, there was a wide cost-of-living difference between Genesee and New York City, but it still took her a moment to find her voice. "That's very generous." And they weren't even his own children.

He shrugged and leaned back against the couch. "I know what Constance paid her housekeeper, and I know the twins. Taking care of Mia and Lucas is more valuable than a housekeeping job. So I upped

Mrs. Harris's salary a bit." Nick held her gaze. "You don't have to let me know right now. Sleep on it."

Ava quickly tallied the positives. It *was* only for four weeks. She'd have several weeks after she finished her summer program before law classes began in late August to possibly get in some temp work at a law firm. She could be choosier about what temp work she'd take. What Nick would pay her would go a long way toward her first semester personal expenses. And accepting Nick's offer would put them in an employer-employee relationship which should keep any attraction to Nick in check.

"No ..."

His chest tightened

She put him out of his misery. "I don't need to sleep on it. I'll take the job with one change. I have a meeting on Thursdays. I can only watch the twins until 4:30."

"It's a deal." Nick rose and extended his hand.

Ava shook his hand. "See you tomorrow at 1:30."

Once she was safely out in the hall, Ava looked up at the ceiling. What had she done? She calmed her dismay. Watching the twins for a few weeks wasn't a detour from her plan. The money she'd earn could help. But shaking your boss's hand wasn't supposed to send a tingle up your arm.

5

———

ick sat at his desk staring out the window, not getting any more work done here in the center's business office than he had at the apartment this morning with the kids. Yesterday afternoon, Ava had taken the twins to the park again. When he'd arrived home from work, she'd given him a quick rundown of their day and said she had to run to meet a classmate at the law library.

It had taken all his control not to ask her if the friend was a male or female. And he wasn't proud of himself for that. Ava was his employee now, along with all the other reasons he'd told himself they shouldn't become involved. Nick picked up a pen and tossed it on the desk. Ava hadn't given any indication to him that she was interested in becoming involved.

"Problem?" Maggie asked.

"Hmmm." He swiveled his chair around toward the office door and the center's manager. Trying to get on his good side after the other day?

"The pen." She moved closer, close enough for him to pick up the scent of her long blonde hair. She had it loose today, rather than the functional braid she typically wore. She leaned over his shoulder for a look at his computer screen. "Anything I can help with."

Yeah, but he couldn't very well say yes, meet me for a drink tonight and help me get a certain college student babysitter out of my head. He studied Maggie while she appeared to study the spreadsheet on the computer.

A slight smile curved her pink-tinged lips.

She knew he'd been checking her out. But she couldn't know he'd been comparing her to Ava. Even though she was his physical type and more his age, Maggie was nowhere near the woman Ava was.

Nick closed the computer window and hit shutdown. "It's six. I'm calling it a day."

Maggie straightened. "I'm off, too. Want to catch a drink?"

"No, thanks. I need to get home to Mia and Lucas." *And find out all about the Firefighters Museum.* Considering the amount of work he didn't get done today, he should have gone with them.

"You can't spare an hour?" Maggie flipped her hair back over her shoulder and gave him what he was sure she thought was a beguiling smile.

It did nothing for him, except make him wonder what it would feel like to get a similar smile from Ava.

"They're with your nanny, right?"

"Ava isn't my nanny. She's ..." What was Ava? "She's a friend, and I wouldn't take advantage of that. She needs her evenings to do her work for the law classes she's taking."

Maggie's shrug irritated him.

"There's other evenings if you change your mind," she said.

"Sorry, I make a point of not dating anyone I work with."

She grimaced. "Whatever." Maggie turned on her heel and left.

Nick gathered what he needed to work at home. Maggie was an attractive woman, an obviously available attractive woman, who didn't hold the least bit of interest for him. Besides. they were more-or-less co-workers, and that was a hard and fast rule for him. A rule that applied even more to Ava, since she worked *for* him. But his rule didn't say they couldn't be friends, as he'd told Maggie. The elevator opened on the 22nd floor. Friends. As he hoped he and Ava were.

Something smelled good when he entered his apartment, but Lucas rushed him before he could ask.

"You should of seed all the fire trucks, Uncle Nick."

He wished he had. "You had fun?"

"The fun-est. We got to climb up and sit in one. You have to come with us next time."

"Next time?" Nick looked over at Ava.

"Lucas thinks we should go every week," she said.

"How about you, Mia. Did you have fun?"

"Yeah, but not as much fun as the playground."

"What smells so good?"

"We made you chocolate chip cookies," Mia said.

"And Ms. Ava made tacos for dinner." Lucas added.

"You didn't have to do that, Ava," Nick said, as he had last night. Although it was great for him to come home to a prepared meal, it wasn't in their work agreement.

Ava waved him off. "Mia and Lucas did most of the work."

"Yeah, Ms. Ava just told us what to do," Mia said.

"And did the stove part," Lucas. "Want me to get you a cookie?"

Nick laughed. Ava joined him. The sound of her laugh mixing with his lower one made his smile widen. "We'd better save the cookies for after dinner, so we don't spoil our appetite."

"Okay," Lucas said. He and his sister ran across the room and climbed up on two of the stools at the counter divider. Plates and flatware had already been set out. For three.

"You're not staying to eat?" Nick asked. She had yesterday.

"No, I have a lot to do this evening."

"The law library again?" A spark of unfounded jealousy over her new friends pricked him.

"Studying at home tonight."

"Take a couple of tacos and a cookie or two with you, so you don't have to spend time cooking." Nick whisked past her into the kitchen to get plastic containers for her food. He took his time to give her a chance to change her mind and eat with them. She had to eat anyway.

"There's only enough for three. I have something quick to fix at home."

"All right," he relented. "See you tomorrow afternoon, and thanks again for cooking."

"You're welcome." Ava walked to the door and stopped. "Remember, I have to leave at 4:30 tomorrow."

"Right. Your meeting." More friends?

When the door closed behind Ava, Nick lifted the platter of tacos from the back of the stove where Ava had been keeping it warm and placed it on the counter. He dished out one taco to each of the twins and two for himself before taking a stool.

"I wish Ms. Ava could eat with us," Mia said between bites.

"She has things to do beside be with us ... you guys," Nick corrected himself.

Lucas nodded. "At her `partment. Have you been there?"

"No." Nick went to the refrigerator to get himself a drink, wondering where the little boy was going with his question. "Do you want some chocolate milk?"

"Yes, please," the kids said together. Ava must be working with them on their manners.

He poured everyone's drinks.

"We have," Mia said.

"Have what?" Nick asked, having lost track of the conversation.

"Have went to Ms. Ava's apartment. To get the chocolate chips. You didn't have any."

"It's bigger than yours with two bedrooms like our old house in Philadelphia. You remember."

Nick remembered only too well. And what did Lucas mean about old house?

"And Ms. Ava has a real table to eat at," Mia said.

"With four chairs. We should move there," Lucas said with a pleased expression.

Nick choked when the water he'd swallowed went down the wrong way. "Did you say that to Ms. Ava?" he got out.

"No," Lucas said.

Nick released the breath he was holding.

"I did," Mia said proudly.

Nick rubbed his chest to relieve the heartburn that had nothing to do with the spicy food.

No wonder Ava couldn't get out of here fast enough.

*A*va was still smiling when she left her apartment for the No Brides Club meeting the next evening, replaying Nick's arrival home in her head. He'd been fifteen minutes early and walked in saying he needed to talk with her privately. Admonishing the twins to sit quietly and watch the Disney DVD she'd put on for them, he'd led her to his bedroom, now obviously the kids' room.

She'd tensed wondering what she must have done wrong. Nothing that she could think of.

Nick had raked one hand through his hair and then stuffed both hands in his front pockets as if he didn't know what to do with them. "Yesterday. The kids," he'd stammered. "Your apartment. They didn't get that idea from me."

"I know," she'd said. She'd spent enough time with Lucas and Mia to know what they were capable of coming up with. Nick should have known that.

Nick's look of relief had been almost comical.

As she peered out the door for the Uber she'd scheduled since it was raining too hard to walk, her smile dimmed with the memory of what had followed. After his brief look of relief, Nick had had to go into a thorough explanation about how they had an employer-employee relationship, and that he would never presume more than that.

Just when she'd thought they were becoming friends. But his words had pretty much cut that thread of thought. Ava had spent the trek to her apartment chiding herself for thinking their relationship could be more. Not romantic, but friendly.

Waiting for her ride, she weighed whether to talk about Nick at the meeting and came down on the side of not mentioning him. She didn't want the other members to think she was weakening on her club vow. She wasn't. Not really. Her ex-fiancé Trey hadn't liked it, but she'd had friendships with guys in high school and college with no romantic intent. Relationships that didn't make major demands on her time as a romantic relationship would.

Ava dashed out when her car arrived. "Briarwood Tavern," she said as she climbed in back and smoothed her casual cotton slacks. Leaning back in the seat for the short ride, Ava ran through what to talk about tonight with the women. The Uber driver hit the brakes hard to avoid a car that had cut in front of them, jerking her against her seatbelt.

"Sorry," the driver said.

"It's okay," she answered absently, deciding to

mainly listen at the meeting, as she'd done last week and answer any questions asked of her. A couple of minutes later, the driver dropped her off in front of the Briarwood. She checked her watch. Right on time this week. They were meeting downstairs, since the weather didn't exactly favor the rooftop bar, where they often met.

She told the hostess that she was meeting friends and pointed to the table where they'd sat last week. Only Brooke, Vivian, Samantha, and Lizzie were there so far.

"Hi," Ava said, taking the seat beside Vivian.

Everyone greeted her.

"We haven't ordered anything yet," Brooke said.

Ava nodded. "Small turnout tonight."

"Yes, Emalie and Marnie should be coming," Lizzie. "Didn't you get the text?"

"What text?" Ava asked.

"That's right," Lizzie said. "You were late last week. We didn't get your cell number for our group text."

"I'll give it to you now." Ava didn't want to admit, even to herself that she was nervous, but she was glad for something to do with her hands, which she couldn't seem to keep still. Everyone pulled out their phones and she recited her number, finishing as a server approached the table.

"Are you ladies ready for drinks?"

"Definitely," Lizzie said. "And we'll take dinner menus, too. We expect two more."

The server passed out the menus she'd brought and started taking drink orders. Ava was the last to order. "I'll try a fresh cherry margarita."

"Ah, channeling Kate," Samantha said. My cousin Julie has said how much your sister likes fresh cherry margaritas.

"She can't stop talking about them, so I might as well see what the attraction is."

Emalie and Marnie had arrived ahead of the others' drinks, so they ordered drinks along with their dinners.

As Ava passed her menu back to the server, she caught sight of Maggie sitting alone frowning at her from the next table.

"Someone from NYU?" Vivian asked.

Ava warmed at her remembering where she was going to school. Vivian must have noticed her staring at Maggie.

The others on Ava's side of the table glanced over.

"Not from school. From the Jansen Athletic Club at my apartment complex. She's the manager. I've done some temp work there this summer. We had an *incident*." Before she knew it, Ava was sharing the run-in with Maggie and her working for Nick, relating the job to her goal of being a children's advocate attorney.

"Some people are so clueless where children are concerned." Brooke said. "I've seen it in my work at the hospital."

"Clueless and also unconcerned at times," Vivian added.

Ava appreciated Brooke and Vivian's support and wasn't surprised by it, since they worked with children as well. But the others all weighed in with their thoughts and professional advice, particularly on managing and dealing with co-workers that related both to the incident with Maggie and her working relationship with Nick.

Ava left the meeting after dinner, feeling like she really belonged to the No Brides Club now. She saw why Kate valued the group so highly.

On her way out with the others, she noticed Maggie still at the next table, getting very cozy with one of the male personal trainers from the athletic club. Obviously, she had no qualms about socializing with her employees. But Ava knew better now after talking with the No Brides Club members that she should put definite boundaries on how friendly she should get with Nick, if at all.

—————

"Right on time," Nick said when he opened the door for Ava on Saturday morning.

"You said 8:30."

He stepped aside, so she could walk in. "Lucas and Mia are loading the breakfast dishes in the dishwasher."

"It's good for them to have household responsibilities."

"I hadn't used the dishwasher when it was just me, but meals for three make a lot more dishes." He laughed. She didn't crack a hint of a smile.

"Mmhmm. Are you working at home or at the athletic club today?" Ava asked.

Before he answered, he studied Ava's totally neutral expression. It was as if someone had replaced the Ava he knew—or thought he knew—with a robotic version. "The club, why?"

"I'll be taking the twins to the Children's Museum when it opens. I have your cell phone number and the club number if I need to reach you for any reason."

Lucas and Mia peered around the counter. "I thought I heard you, Ms. Ava," Mia said.

For the first time, Ava smiled. At the twins. It shouldn't matter. But it did. He was actually jealous—the only way he could describe what he was feeling—of her smile for Mia and Lucas.

"Come see." Lucas trotted over and grabbed her hand and tugged her to the kitchen area. "We did the dishes."

"Nice work." Ava's two words to the kids had far more enthusiasm in them than everything she'd said to him that morning combined.

"I'll get going, then. Who has a hug for me?"

Lucas and Mia ran over and almost tackled him.

"You guys do what Ms. Ava tells you," he said after hugging each of them. He glanced over at her, and Ava's unreadable gaze caught his until he released the twins and broke it.

"We will," Mia and Lucas said. His heart warmed. They tried.

Somehow the air in the hall when he stepped out seemed lighter, more breathable. He headed down to the club.

"Good morning, Mr. Jansen," the person on the front desk said as he passed by.

"Good morning," he replied. "Any messages?"

"Yes, I almost forgot. Mr. Jansen, the other Mr. Jansen, called this morning. He wants you to call him."

"Thanks." Uncle Pete had already called this morning? Nick glanced up at the clock. It wasn't as if he was in late, and his uncle had his cell number. He shook off the feeling that his uncle's message meant he'd somehow found him lacking. That was only Ava. He was uneasy only after Ava's robotic actions around him.

"Hi," Maggie said from her desk before he'd even crossed the threshold to the business office.

"Hi." He wasn't prepared to fend off Maggie this morning.

"I'm glad you came in. There's something I want to talk with you about."

Nick put his briefcase and laptop on the desk he was using. Good. It sounded like business.

"I'm not sure it's my business."

Then it probably isn't.

"I met a friend at the Briarwood Tavern last night." Maggie paused. "I saw your nanny there with a group of women."

Nick refrained from correcting the nanny part in hopes of getting Maggie to spit out whatever she had to say. "Ava had a meeting there last night," he finally said into the silence.

"If that's the case..." Maggie laughed. "I'd say the purpose of the meeting was to get drunk."

Nick swallowed his distaste for workplace gossip. A hangover could explain why Ava had acted strangely this morning. When he was twenty-three, he was a lot less responsible than Ava seemed to be. "You're right. It's none of your business." Nick shot down Maggie's gossip and received a sour look in return.

The phone on his desk rang. It never rang. "Excuse me," Nick said, glad for a reason to dismiss Maggie. He picked up the receiver and moved to his chair behind the desk.

"Nick Jansen," he said.

"Nick, Uncle Pete. You got my message?"

"Yes, I just got in and was about to call you." he glanced at the clock on the phone. It was just 9:00.

"I need you to come here to Buffalo."

"Is there a problem with the facility there?" Nothing had popped out in his preliminary review of the club there.

"Not at all. I think it's my best run club."

Probably because Uncle Pete was there to pop in unexpectedly.

"It's your Aunt Sandra's birthday. The whole family will be here. I thought we could mix business and pleasure. I can show you the Buffalo club. It's how I'd like the New York one to operate, too, once I've moved them into the nonprofit, and have you and the other nonprofit board members in place. And you can reacquaint yourself with and meet the rest of my family."

"When?"

"Next Saturday. We're having a barbeque. I realize it's a holiday weekend, but I thought we'd get together Friday to talk business."

"Can I get back to you on that?" Nick explained his situation with Lucas and Mia and having to make arrangements for them to stay with Ava, if she was agreeable.

"Bring the girlfriend and your kids along. Friday is the Fourth of July. I'm sure she won't have law classes. I'll get you a hotel room for the weekend. We'll be full up here with all the kids and grandkids."

Nick heard someone calling his uncle in the background. "I'll let you know later today."

"Fine. I've got to go." His uncle clicked off.

Nick placed the receiver back on the phone and stared at it. And he'd set Uncle Pete straight on the situation with Ava and the twins—and the hotel room. He should have right off. But his uncle started talking about his family. And the party for his aunt sounded like the family gatherings his high school friends had complained about having to go to. The family parties he'd envied after his father had died. His mother was an only child of only children and had cut off all contact with his father's family after his death.

In that moment, he'd bought into the fantasy of Ava and the twins being his family.

How sad was that?

"I understand if you don't want to take the twins for an entire weekend," Nick said when he'd finished telling her about the business meeting with his uncle in Buffalo and the family party."

"No, it's not that." Ava bit her lip while she came up with words that wouldn't make her sound like a homesick teen, away for the first time. She released her lip when she realized Nick was staring at her mouth. She cleared her throat. "I was thinking that my parents live in a town on the way to Buffalo, and I'm sure the twins would love visiting and staying at a working farm."

Nick glanced over the counter dividing the living room and kitchen.

Checking to see if Mia and Lucas were listening? She was sure they were too engrossed in the computer game they were playing on her laptop.

"Your parents have a farm?"

"Yes, dairy."

He studied her so intently that her fingers began to tingle.

"They would love to visit a farm."

His wide grin made her think he might be almost as pumped.

"Not just visit. The kids and I could stay there. You, too," she added. "There's plenty of room."

"Your parents wouldn't mind? It would be less than a week's notice."

Ava laughed. "To have kids in the house again, even for just a couple of days? An hour would be enough notice."

"Seriously?" The only word for Nick's expression was astounded.

"Seriously. And with Mia and Lucas there, I'll be an adult, not the family baby. My brother and sister are eleven and almost thirteen years older than I am. I was an oops baby." Ava blushed at the way the excitement of a visit home was making her babble on.

"But the twins aren't related to them, your parents."

"They aren't related to you, either."

"True. But I'd have to give my mother a month's notice, and she'd probably get us a hotel room."

"Like your uncle offered?"

"No, Uncle Pete said he'd invite us to stay at his place if he didn't have my cousins and their families staying there for my aunt's birthday."

Ava took the way Nick jumped right in to defend his uncle to mean something, although she wasn't entirely sure what. It also made her realize how little she knew about Nick beyond his situation with the kids and the professional information about him that she'd picked up online.

"I quit!" Mia's exclamation interrupted Ava and Nick's conversation. "Lucas is winning because he can remember more letters."

Ava struggled to keep a straight face. The object of the game was to type the letter or combination of letters that fell from the cloud before they hit the ground. She rose onto her tiptoes, leaned toward Nick and whispered in his ear, "Someone didn't take an n-a-p, and someone else did."

As she nodded over her shoulder toward Lucas who was still engrossed in the game, her cheek rubbed against his jawline stubble. Ava jumped back as if burned.

Nick tilted his head and the corner of his mouth twitched.

He must think she'd never felt the brush of a man's whiskers against her skin. Of course, she had. She'd been engaged to Trey. But whiskers, even Trey's, had never ignited the charge that had run through her just now and settled still vibrating in her stomach.

"I'll, um, go home and call Mom."

"You do that," Nick, said, mouth corners still twitching.

With a quick "bye" to the twins, Ava fled into the hall. She leaned her back to the wall beside his apartment door and took a deep breath. Nick was the first man she'd been attracted to since her broken engagement. She was going to have to work hard to keep their relationship in the friend zone and to keep her no brides vow.

In her apartment, she dropped to the couch and pulled her cell phone from her bag.

"Hi," her mother answered her call.

"Hi."

"How are your classes going?"

"Great." It was just the rest of her life that was in a jumble.

"Kate said that you have a part-time job, too. I hope you're not taking on too much."

Ava bit her tongue, thinking *Mom wouldn't have asked Kate that.* "No, not at all. It's a childcare job. Twin five-year-olds. More fun than work." As the words came out, she realized that taking care of Mia and Lucas was fun—down time from the intensity of her classes.

Her mother laughed. "Only you would say that."

"So are you and Dad busy next weekend?"

"Nothing planned. Why?"

"The guy I'm working for has to come to Buffalo for a business meeting on Friday."

"On the fourth of July?"

"It's a family business. Anyway, when he asked me to take the kids, I suggested we come instead and stay with you."

"Sure, we certainly have the room."

"I told him, it wasn't any problem, and I think the kids will love staying on a farm. They're used to living in a big city. We'll try to get out of here right after my Thursday class, around two. So look for us about 7:30-8."

"We will. I know it's only been a few weeks since you left, but it will be so good to see you."

"You and Dad, too. Bye."

Ava fixed herself a sandwich for supper and jumped into her class assignment to give Nick some time to feed and get the twins settled before she called him about next weekend. The study time wouldn't hurt her efforts to get her mind back on the career track, either. Before she knew it, it was past 9:00. She grabbed her phone and pressed Nick's number. The phone rang so long, she expected to be redirected to his voice mail, which would be fine. She could leave him the information. In fact, that would be better.

"Hello."

Ava waited a moment to see if Nick had answered or she'd get the rest of his voicemail message. "Hi, I didn't know if I'd gotten you or the beginning of your voicemail message."

"It's me. I'm embarrassed to say that after I got the twins to bed, I sat in the recliner for a minute before I dug into my work, and I fell asleep."

His follow-up laugh rippled through her. "Oh, sorry I woke you. I could have left you a message." From the effect his laugh had had on her, she wished she could have left a message.

"No, I do have a couple work things I need to do tonight."

"So we're all set with my parents. I told Mom we'd leave as soon as possible after I get home from class and to expect us about 7:30-8."

"You think it will take us that long? I figured here to Buffalo would take no more than about six hours. And didn't you say your parents live on the way to Buffalo?"

"They do. But your estimate doesn't account for traveling with kids. You have to figure in an hour for supper at one of the Thruway rest stops, and a bathroom break or two."

"You're the expert. I've never traveled a long distance with Mia and Lucas, and my mother and I didn't take car trips."

"What, no fun-filled family summer vacations?" she teased.

"Nope. I went to camp all summer by bus, or train, or plane."

"Oh" was all she could say.

"She didn't believe in family vacations. They might take her focus off work and the next step up the corporate ladder."

His bitter tone hit her like a pail of ice water and made her heart ache for the child-Nick. She'd never do that to a child. One more reason to stick with her career-goal first, then marriage and family later. It avoided such a conflict.

"Well, friend, our upcoming trip to the Lewis family farm should be a real treat for you, too."

"I'm sure it will be. I'd better get to work. See you tomorrow."

"Right. Bye."

She stared at her phone until it went back to the home screen. Her putting their relationship into words and being with other people next weekend should help her distance herself from Nick on any plane other than friendship.

———

"Is it time for Ms. Ava to be back from school yet?" Mia asked five minutes after Lucas had asked the same question and right on schedule with their asking him every twenty minutes. If this was a preview of the drive to Western New York, he was about ready to take back the rental SUV they'd picked up earlier this morning and buy them all plane tickets. Hang the cost of not buying tickets in advance. The flight time averaged only about fifty-seven minutes. He knew because he'd looked it up an hour ago.

"Not yet. Remember, I showed you on the DVR clock. Ms. Ava won't be home and ready to go until the clock says two-o-o."

"But what if the electricity goes off?" Lucas asked.

Nick scratched his head. "What if?"

"Then the clock won't show any numbers, and we won't know when Ms. Ava will be here."

Nick had to admit that that was pretty good reasoning for a five-year-old. "But my cell phone won't go off if we lose electricity." He placed his phone on the TV stand and showed them how to press the home button and get the time. "Every time you think about asking me if it's time yet, press the button and find out yourself."

"So we don't bother you while you're working," Lucas said.

Nick had given up any realistic idea of getting real work done hours ago. If he could get Lucas and Mia to watch one of the videos they'd brought with them, he might be able to get the report his uncle had sent him this morning read.

"I'll make you a deal," he said. "You can watch

one of your videos if you check the time Ms. Ava should get here yourselves and don't ask me."

"Okay," Lucas said, pushing the cell phone button and looking at the screen. "It's not time yet."

"No, it's not." Their reporting on the time every five minutes wouldn't be much better than their asking what time it was. "And don't tell me until it's time. I want to be surprised."

Mia sighed. "All right. We'll watch a video."

Nick turned the DVR on. "I'll be in the bedroom at my desk," which he hadn't used since the twins took over his room. "And I can see you through the doorway."

"Okay, Uncle Nick," the twins chorused

After a short argument from the other room about which video to watch, things quieted, and Nick started reading the report. Then it began.

"One-three-six," Lucas announced over the video sound.

"One-three-eight," Mia reported.

"One-four-one." Lucas again.

Nick covered his ears.

"Uncle Nick, someone is at the door," Mia shouted.

Crash!

Nick pushed away from the desk and sprinted

through the doorway, where Mia looked up at him from the hardwood floor.

"I tripped on the lamp cord." A table lamp was smashed beside her.

He scooped her up and examined her. "Are you okay?"

"Yes, but someone is still knocking at the door. What if it's Ms. Ava, and she thinks we left without her?"

"It's not two-o-o yet," Lucas said.

Nick placed Mia back on the floor and unplugged the lamp before joining them at the door. He looked out the peep hole. "You're right. It's Ms. Ava." He opened the door. "I'm so happy you're here, I could hug you."

Ava stopped mid-step through the doorway.

Of course, he wouldn't. Couldn't. Although now he was wondering what it would feel like to have Ava in his arms.

"Come on in."

He closed the door and followed her gaze to the broken lamp Lucas now crouched next to. "Don't touch anything," he warned.

"Interesting morning?" Ava asked.

"You could say that."

"Ms. Ava." Lucas was back by the TV. It's one-five-two. Uncle Nick said you would be here at two-o-o."

"I see. Should I go to my apartment and come back then?"

Ava and Nick burst out laughing when Mia and Lucas shouted, "No."

"I'll clean up the lamp, and we can get going. Is that all your luggage?" He pointed at the small pull-along bag by the door.

"That's it. We're only going for the weekend."

Nick's case wasn't any larger, but Constance would have had at least twice as much luggage for a weekend trip.

In the parking garage, Nick put Ava's case in the back of the SUV he'd rented, while Ava got the kids strapped into their booster seats.

"We're on our way," Ava said when they pulled out of the parking garage. "What do you want to see first on the farm tomorrow?"

"You're taking us to a farm?" Lucas asked.

"With horses and cows and chickens?" Mia added to his question.

"And a tractor and other `quipment?" Lucas got in before Ava could answer.

"We're staying at my parent's house. They live on a farm, with all those things, except horses."

"Cool," Lucas said.

"Uncle Nick didn't tell us."

"I wanted it to be a surprise," he said. *And I didn't want to be bombarded with a hundred questions I couldn't answer.* Nick leaned back in his seat, relaxed and mellowed by the happy cadence in Ava's voice as she told the twins stories of growing up on a farm.

He was seeing a different facet of her. A side he liked as much as the childcare-giver-law-student side he'd seen in New York. And, although he knew better, Nick couldn't deny to himself that he'd like to know more—everything there was—about her.

———

"That supper stop did the trick." Ava turned back around to face forward in the car. "They're both fast asleep."

"As am I, almost, with all the quiet. Could you hand me my coffee?"

Ava picked up the extra-large, sugar, no cream coffee from the console cupholder. His fingers brushed hers as she passed the cup to him. She released it and flexed her hand against the heat that was still spreading across her palm and up her arm. "That's a hot cup of coffee," she said to quash her thought that it wasn't the cup of coffee that had generated the heat.

The barely contained smile on Nick's face said that her statement had sounded as lame as she thought it had.

"So do you have any more farm stories to keep me awake and entertained?" he asked.

"No, enough about me." *More than enough. Way more.* "It's your turn."

"Okay, what would you like to know?"

"Where did you grow up?"

"Philadelphia."

Ava waited for him to continue. "Come on. You can do better than that, after all the information I spilled." Her cheeks warmed. With her avid audience, she *had* run on and hoped she hadn't spouted anything too embarrassing. "You could give me a little more detail. Right in the city? In the suburbs?"

"Right in the city."

Another difference between them. But she was learning to appreciate some of the benefits of city living.

Nick's hand tightened on the steering wheel. "My mother has a house on Delaney Place in the Rittenhouse Square area."

He'd said that like it should mean something.

"I'm not familiar with Philadelphia." Although she *could* Google the neighborhood, she'd rather hear about it from Nick. And why was he so reticent about talking about himself? Wasn't get-the-man-talking-about-himself the number one rule for breaking the ice on a first date? Not that this was anything remotely close to a date. But she was interested in Nick—as a friend.

"It's a Mainline neighborhood. Mother has a brownstone she inherited from her parents."

Nick's reference to his mother as Mother, and not my mother didn't escape her. "And your father?"

"Died in an accident when I was six. He was an international freelance photographer. He was usually gone on a shoot." Nick set his jaw.

"How about some radio?" she asked.

"Good idea."

Ava pressed the search button on the car radio, her finger itching to pull her phone out and search for information on Nick's parents. She didn't know what had her so curious, except the fact that growing up in a small town, she'd known the families of nearly anyone she met. Their people, as her grandmother had always said. The radio scanned and settled on a Rochester oldies station.

"Hope you like oldies, or country. West of Utica, that's mostly your choices."

"I can live with oldies, although jazz is my preference."

Score one for her. Nick had shared some personal information without her digging it out of him. She settled back in her seat with her head leaning on the headrest.

"Hey, you're not going to sleep on me, too, are you?"

"No, I'm only relaxing."

A couple of minutes later, Nick broke the silence. "I'm not close to my family, like you are."

"I picked up on that."

He laughed.

"One more question. The uncle you're working with, maternal or paternal?"

"Paternal. My mother is an only child of only children."

From his profile, she almost missed the sheepish expression that crossed his face before he spoke.

"The barbeque thing on Saturday. Aside from Uncle Pete, you'll know the people there about as well as I will."

Ava's chest tightened at the oh-so-slight quiver in Nick's voice. Before moving to New York, Ava had thought she could readily fit into any group. Almost everyone she knew back home remarked on or criticized how social she was. "Good thing we'll have Mia and Lucas to break the ice," she said.

"I knew they were good for something," Nick said.

"You don't mean that."

"Of course, I don't. I love those two as if they were my own—as well as I can."

Ava wondered what he meant by his last comment, but something in the way Nick held himself after saying it, stopped her from asking. She looked out the side window. "We're coming up on the Montezuma Wildlife Preserve. Have you ever been there?"

"No I haven't."

Ava told him a story about her middle school Girl Scout troop hiking through the preserve, finishing off with, "Were you a Boy Scout?"

"Yes, an Eagle Scout."

"I'm impressed."

"Just following my mother's motto, don't do something unless you're willing to put in the effort to be the best at it."

"You must have tried a thing or two just for fun, even if you weren't that good at it?"

"Not really."

Ava shook her head, laughing. "If I'd done that, it would have cut my social life by a third." Nick wasn't laughing with her, or even smiling. "You were serious."

"I'm afraid so. I've always tried to encourage Mia and Lucas to experiment, to try different things and have always found something positive to compliment about their effort. I may have been too successful with Mia and experimenting. The kids had it rough the first couple years of their life. For any faults I have with Constance, her getting custody of Mia and Lucas was the best thing that could have happened to them."

"And you," Ava whispered, as much to herself as to Nick.

The radio started crackling and breaking up. Ava reached forward and pressed scan, and a clear station came in.

"Jazz," Nick said. "About time we heard some good music."

"It must be a Rochester station," Ava commented. "And there was nothing wrong with my previous choices, given what was available." She leaned back and closed her eyes. "I'm listening to the music, not falling asleep." *And taking advantage of the break in the conversation.* The more she wrangled out of Nick, the more she liked him and wanted to know more.

Not too long after, Nick exited the interstate.

"A sleepy-sounding Mia asked from the back seat, "Are we almost there?"

Nick looked to Ava for the answer.

"Yes, we're about twenty miles from my mom and dad's. Turn left at the exit light. We'll go through a little bit of Batavia and two small villages before we go up a hill on Route 98 to the farm."

"How long?" Lucas wanted to know.

"About twenty minutes?" Nick asked in a low voice.

"No more like about forty minutes. We will be on local roads from Batavia on."

"When is forty minutes on the clock, Ms. Ava?" Lucas asked.

She looked to Nick.

"I was teaching them time—sort of—to keep them busy this morning. The clock will say seven-four-o."

"Okay, Lucas said."

"About as long as the *Bob the Builder* video we watched at the Kids Korner that day."

"That's pretty long," Mia whined.

"But it'll be worth it. My mother texted me while you were sleeping. She baked brownies for you and made ice cream from our own cows' milk."

"Your mother knows how to make ice cream?" Mia's voice bounced around the inside of the car.

"She does. But she only makes it for special people and special occasions."

"Which are we?" Lucas asked.

"Both," Nick answered before Ava could.

"I can't wait until we get there," Lucas said. "It's seven-o-six now."

Ava turned forward in her seat. She couldn't wait, either, to see her parents, and being in her childhood home would put a buffer between her and Nick. If he did one more lovable thing before they got there...

Lovable? Where had that come from? She had it worse than she'd thought.

7

———

*N*ick placed his razor on the bathroom sink, looked in the mirror, and splashed water on his face to remove the last of the shaving cream. He couldn't believe it. Bonnie and Tim Lewis were as welcoming as Ava had said. After stuffing them with snacks last night, Tim had helped him check his directions to his uncle's Buffalo club, while Bonnie had offered to tuck the twins in their room and read them a story. She'd also told Mia and Lucas they could call her Nana Bonnie, which set off some warning signals in his head. He'd have to take Ava aside and talk with her.

He stepped out of the bathroom, buttoning his dress shirt. He spotted Ava taking the twins downstairs.

"Mom has breakfast ready," Ava said over her shoulder.

He quickly finished buttoning his shirt when he felt Ava's gaze on him. Or imagined it. He *did* try to keep himself in shape. "I'll be right down," he said to her retreating back.

"Good morning," Bonnie said. "Sit. I'll have another stack of pancakes ready in a minute."

The only available seat was next to Ava. The other empty seat, next to her father, had a half mug of coffee by it. "Good morning." He pulled out the chair next to Ava. Of course that's where Bonnie had him seated. He was Ava's guest.

"Nana Bonnie, these are the bestest pancakes ever," Lucas said.

There was that, too. Nick looked at the kitchen clock. He'd have to put off that talk with Ava until after he got back from his meeting.

"Thank you, Lucas," Bonnie said.

"Yeah, we only have the kind from the toaster," Mia said.

"You didn't have to go to all this trouble for us," Nick said, feeling he should say something.

Bonnie placed a platter of pancakes in front of him. "It's a holiday. I would have made something special for the two of us anyway. Ava, can you get Nick a cup of coffee?"

"I can get my own coffee." Nick put three pancakes on his plate and started to push his chair back.

Ava was already standing. "No problem. I'll get it." She filled a mug from the coffee maker on the counter behind her and placed the mug in front of his plate.

The aroma of the coffee mingled with a fainter aroma of maple syrup, and a light flowery scent he'd come to associate with Ava.

"Here's the sugar." She handed him the sugar bowl.

"Thanks." She'd remembered. His stomach flip-flopped. He didn't know why his insides were making a big deal about such a small thing as remembering how he took his coffee. Nick added butter and syrup to his pancakes and sliced off a large bite, savoring the taste of the syrup and the texture of the pancakes.

"Papa Tim—" Mia started.

Nick's mouthful of pancake got stuck in his throat. He swallowed hard, glancing up and down the table to see if anyone had noticed. *Nope.* He was safe.

"He makes the syrup from trees, instead of buying it from the store," Mia finished with a giggle.

"Not from trees," Lucas corrected her. "From sap that comes from trees. With buckets."

"Whatever." Mia shrugged.

"Papa Tim is going to show us his cows later," Lucas said. "He already got up early and milked them with his helpers. While we were still sleeping. He has milking `quipment he's going to show me, too."

Something mechanical. Lucas's favorite. "That sounds like fun" *It did.*

"Want us to wait until you get back from your meeting, Uncle Nick?" Lucas asked. "You and Ms. Ava could come, too."

He wanted to. But his meeting was important. For his business and, he realized, for him, too. His uncle Pete was actually his family. Family he hadn't seen in more than twenty years. His mother had said his father's family didn't want to have anything to do with them after his father had died. Which, after talking to Uncle Pete, didn't ring true. Not wanting to create conflict, Nick had taken his mother at her word and hadn't pursued contact. He'd pretty much locked any thought of his father's family into the past. His experience with family didn't recommend the institution.

"What do you think, Uncle Nick?" Lucas prompted.

"When did Mr. Lewis say he'd show you."

"After lunch."

He nodded and Ava added, "So they might n-a-p when they come back."

"That means nap," Mia said. "Nana Bonnie told us last night."

"I'm sorry," Bonnie said with a crooked smile he'd seen on Ava's face before. "After their story last night, they were telling me the words they know, and Mia asked what n-a-p spelled. I answered before thinking."

"That's okay." It was done now. He and Ava could switch to s-l-e-e-p, but he had a strong feeling they'd figure the word out immediately. "I'll tell you what I'll do. I'll try to be back for lunch. If I'm not, go ahead without me."

"O-kay," Lucas said. "If you don't get back in time, maybe Papa Tim will show you tomorrow."

"That sounds like a plan," Nick said.

"Now," Ava said. "Why don't you let your uncle eat and come upstairs with me to get washed up and dressed."

Ava and the twins left as did Tim, who needed to

finish his morning work in the barn. Nick suspected Tim was making his getaway now so he wouldn't have two little helpers tagging along.

Nick gripped the handle of the coffee mug tight. That left him and Ava's mother. He took a gulp of coffee and a deep breath to ready himself for the questioning.

"Ava said you're a business consultant."

Here they came. "Yes, primarily for sales or purchases. I worked at a firm in Philadelphia in mergers and acquisitions before I went out on my own."

"It sounds interesting. Businesses would include farms?"

Ava's parents wanted to sell out?

"Not us," Bonnie laughed,

His expression must have given him away.

"But a lot of area farms may not last beyond our generation. The kids don't want to take them on. We're lucky. We own and work the farm with Tim's brother and his son. We all have a buyout agreement with our nephew when we want to retire."

"That sounds like a solid plan." Nick dug into his last pancake with a silent *whew*. For a moment, he thought she might grill him for free advice.

"But ..."

Nick braced himself.

"The local Cooperative Extension might be interested in having you come and talk. Think about it. Now, I'd better let you finish eating."

"I will. To both."

Dishes clanked as Bonnie loaded the dishwasher, drawing Nick's attention to Ava's mother. He watched her bustle around, cleaning up. Ava looked a lot like her mother, who was an attractive woman for, what, fifty-five ... sixty? As he sipped the last of his coffee, an adage he'd heard somewhere popped into his mind. *Look at her mother and you'll see your future.* From here, that future didn't look bad. Not bad at all.

Nick's coffee mug dropped to the table with a thud. He'd tightened his grip at the last moment to stop it from crashing to the table. What was with him? He had no plans to be with Ava in twenty or thirty years—only until the twins went back to Constance. Then they'd simply be neighbors. And when he finished the athletic club job, he'd go back home to Philadelphia.

He studied the design on the coffee mug as if his life depended on it. So why did the prospect of going home make his stomach muscles clench? And why did the fact that Ava's mother was a pleasant, likable, attractive woman reassure him?

———

"You know taking on two five-year-olds is a big commitment," Ava's mother said as the two of them watched her father walking Mia and Lucas to the barn. Her mother had jumped on his offer to do the tour alone, saying she and Ava needed some "girl" time.

Ava had been keeping herself busy with the twins to avoid that.

"Taking care of the twins hasn't been bad, and the job's only for a couple more weeks until they go back to their mother." Ava stopped rather than trying to say more around the lump that had lodged itself in her throat at the thought of not seeing Mia and Lucas, maybe ever again.

"Oh, I thought they were Nick's and you and Nick were ... Well, remember when your sister brought Jon to your graduation party."

"I'm not Kate, and Nick and I aren't whatever you were thinking. Once the kids are gone, I'll be devoting myself 100% to law school. And my No Brides Club vow."

Her mother made a face. Mom had been skeptical of the group since Kate had first told her—before Kate had fallen in love with Jon *and* achieved her career goal.

"Back to the kids. I don't recall them mentioning their mother once since they've been here."

"They don't talk about her to me much, either. It's sad, isn't it? The woman who has custody of the twins is actually an aunt who took them after Social Services removed them from her sister."

"Then, how does Nick have them?"

"Constance, their guardian, is Nick's ex-fiancée. She's on a month-long honeymoon with her new husband." Ava explained how Constance had just dropped the kids on him. "They're very attached to him."

"I noticed. I also noticed he's quite a bit older than you."

And how had she done that? Ava didn't even know for sure how old Nick was.

"From what he said about his work, he must be more Josh's age or even Kate's."

Ava puffed blowing her bangs from her forehead. "And what does my boss's age have to do with anything?"

"Your involvement with the twins and him ... he seems like more than a boss."

"Okay, we're neighbors, friends. That's it." Her face flushed. Mom was going to think she was denying the truth.

"I don't want you hurt again. You put off transferring from community college and finishing your bachelor's degree because you and Trey wanted to get married. Then he broke it off."

"And I was hurt." She'd never told her mother Trey had broken their engagement because she'd become boring. Now she was working on not being boring. She couldn't tell her that either. It would sound too flighty.

Her mother put her had up. "Let me finish. You raced through your bachelor's degree and on to law school. Now the first friend you've made in New York is Nick."

"Not true," Ava interrupted. "I have the women Kate introduced me to, especially Vivian, who's an elementary school teacher, and Brooke, who's an oncology nurse at Children's Hospital." Not that she spent anywhere near as much time with them as she did with Nick.

"I'm sorry. You're my baby. I want to protect you. I can't help thinking about all the times you were gung-ho on something and switched mid-stream. Remember, you originally wanted to be a kindergarten teacher, but changed your mind to preschool teacher when you and Trey started to get serious."

"I've done a lot of growing up—fast—since then. I'm serious about becoming an attorney advocate for children."

"I know you think that. But I worry you're trying to be too much like Kate and are going to lose yourself."

Meaning Mom thinks I can't do it. "How about I promise I won't, and we drop the subject and we take care of the lunch dishes."

"Deal, for now. But I'm never going to stop being your mother."

"I can't argue with that. But I'm your adult baby now."

Her mother sighed. "I suppose you're right."

"Maybe Kate will give you grandchildren soon."

"I can only hope."

"I'll hope with you."

Her mother's expression turned sheepish. "Last night when we all were together in the living room, a part of me, a small part, kind of wished you and Nick were a thing, so I'd get those adorable children as grandchildren."

"Better put your hopes back on Kate. I've got at least three, or more, years before I can even begin to think in that direction. Having a serious relationship, that is."

"Nor would I push you to." Her mother picked up a plate from the table. "I'll take care of the dishes. You can go out in the garden and pick some more strawberries, since you were the one who promised the twins my strawberry shortcake for supper dessert."

"I really wanted it for myself. With your homemade biscuits, it's the best. I've never found any better."

"That flattery and a bowl of fresh strawberries will get you everywhere with me."

Ava laughed and got a strainer out of the cupboard. "I'll be right back."

Out in the garden searching the second crop strawberry plants for fruit, Ava congratulated herself for getting through to her mother some about her dedicating the next few years to establishing her career. What she couldn't understand was why she didn't feel more upbeat about her success.

———

he shortcut Tim had given him in the route to Uncle Pete's club had gotten him there faster than he'd expected, even though it had seemed to be a roundabout way. So he had a breather to mentally prepare himself for meeting with his uncle. He shouldn't be nervous. He and Uncle Pete had talked countless times on the phone, and he'd handled far larger deals when he'd been in mergers and acquisitions. The only factor that he'd come up with that was different was that this meeting was with family.

Nick grabbed his briefcase and got out of the car. Before going in, he assessed the outside of the club and the parking lot, as he assessed the appearance of the neighborhood he'd driven through to get here. From what he'd seen the area and the building were attractive, well kept, and easily accessible. Points that would contribute to the club's continuing success, which had Nick wondering why Uncle Pete was keeping it out of the sale. If it was nostalgia because it was also his uncle's first club, that was something Nick wanted to discuss.

"Good morning. Welcome to the Jansen Athletic Club," the perky blonde behind the check in desk said, giving him a once over that fed his masculine ego, but earned a demerit in his assessment of the club.

"Sorry about that. You *have* to be Pete's nephew. You look just like him, only thirty years younger."

Nice save. He'd see about that. "Yes, Nick Jansen. Can you let him know I'm here?"

"He said to send you right down. Take the hallway to my left. You'll see the business office."

"Thanks." Nick noted that so far, the layout of this club matched the one in Tribeca. Maybe they all had the same design, something he should have known.

He knocked at the business office door and opened it at the "come in" he'd received and stopped dead. The man rising from his seat behind a desk looked exactly as he imagined his father would have had he lived. He couldn't remember his uncle looking like his father when Nick was a child. But he'd only been six the last time he'd seen either of them, and his father had spent much of his time away on assignments.

"You look like Dad." The words in his head escaped his mouth.

Nick regrouped and approached the desk, taking the seat across from his uncle.

"I'm not surprised. We were twins. Fraternal, not identical, though."

"I didn't know that." There was so much he didn't know about the Jansens.

"And now you have twins." Uncle Pete smiled.

"Not exactly." Nick explained the situation with the twins and Ava.

"Somehow, I knew you were the man for this job. Both parts of the job: selling my business and helping me fulfill my long-time dream of personally doing something to help disadvantaged youth by setting up a nonprofit organization to operate free athletic clubs just for them."

Uncle Pete's dream. Nick heard his mother's voice saying "the Jansens are all dreamers," with the implication they could be more successful if they didn't let their dreams get in the way of their careers. To Nick, it looked like his uncle was both. He'd had business success and a dream.

"Pardon?" He'd been so lost in the past that he'd missed what Uncle Pete had said.

"I sensed you could handle the whole job, and the twins prove it. How many men would have stepped in as you did, during your engagement and now?"

"I love the twins."

His uncle slapped the desk. "Exactly. You care, as Dan did. Excuse the criticism, but I'm glad to see that your mother didn't drum that out of you. You probably didn't know, but the wildlife photos he took when he was between news assignments ..."

"I remember the animal pictures." Nick's father had put together an album of the photos that he still had.

"Dan gave any sales proceeds and royalties he earned on them to wildlife preservation and animal rescue organizations. He toyed with the idea of someday starting his own animal rescue."

Unpleasant memories flooded him. Arguments between his parents that he hadn't understood as a child. Mother telling Dad that he was wasting his time taking wildlife photos, deriding Dad for turning down a news assignment shortly before he left on the wildlife shoot, where he'd died in a car accident.

"Sorry," his uncle said. "I got off track there."

"It's fine. It reminds me how little I know about my father." How little his mother had shared with him when he was growing up. Dad had been almost a taboo subject.

"Let's get on with the tour, then. Afterwards I'll tell you more about my idea for converting the

Tribeca and Buffalo clubs."

"Sound good. I'll get my tablet out for notes."

Two hours later, Uncle Pete walked Nick to the club exit.

His uncle gave him a man-hug. "You've got the directions to our place. Come tomorrow any time after noon."

"We'll be there, and I'll get right on the things we discussed."

"Not until you're back in the office Monday. Enjoy your stay in the country."

"I'll try, but our meeting has me jazzed about the job."

His uncle smiled and shook his head. "I remember being young and hungry for success. It'll come just as fast if you take a day or two off to fill the well."

Nick didn't contradict his uncle, even though he wasn't 100% on board with him. He waved goodbye as he pulled out. He wouldn't make it back to Genesee in time for the twins after-lunch farm tour, but it was time well spent. Not only had he gotten all the facts he needed to go full steam ahead on both the sale valuation and his part of setting up the nonprofit, he had gotten a sense of belonging. Uncle Pete, and the rest of his father's family, *had* wanted to stay close with him, and his mother had rebuffed every overture. The final break had been when Mother had returned Uncle Pete's college graduation gift, making it look as if Nick had returned it. After that, Uncle Pete had stopped trying.

He merged onto the interstate, thinking it was surprising he wasn't more messed up than he was in forming relationships with others. Maybe, there was some hope for him.

His pulse thrummed. For him *and* Ava?

8

"And after the barn, Papa Tim took us for a tractor ride," Lucas said

"One at a time," Ava clarified for Nick, so he wouldn't picture the two of them hanging off her father and the tractor. Afterall, she was in charge of the twins and keeping them safe when they were with her.

She shuddered at a remembrance of things Kate and Josh had told her they'd done as kids not much older than Mia and Lucas. Either their parents had gotten stricter with Ava or she simply hadn't had the sense of adventure her older siblings had had. Most likely the second. Kate had glided right into her college courses and living in New York City. She'd been right at home—her new home—within two weeks. It struck Ava that it might have been unwise to come home for a visit so soon.

But Nick had needed her. He was so engrossed in the twins, she could study him without him noticing. He had a twin on each knee and a look of such joy gazing down at them that she felt like an intruder and had to look away. *If only he'd look at her like that.* Ava closed her eyes. That thought had to have come from her mother's talk with her and her homesickness. *But not entirely.* Ava wasn't so naïve she didn't consider that part of her thought came from her heart.

She gazed at his back. Nick *was* attractive. And not only in the physical sense of broad shoulders, a toned build, handsome features, and a quick and interesting mind. But also in his kind personality. She had no doubt he could be a killer in the boardroom. But from what she had seen, he could leave work at work. Had that come after he'd achieved career success? She didn't think she had the capacity to do that right now. She always threw herself into whatever was her current focus completely.

"What did you think, Mia?" Nick asked.

Ava shut down her internal thoughts to listen. Mia had been unusually quiet.

"I liked the tractor ride."

"What about the cows?"

"They're awfully big." Mia hesitated before saying in a small voice. "I got scared. Papa Tim had to pick me up."

"I told her it was okay," Lucas said, patting his sister's knee. "I get scared of things, too, just different things."

"Good man," Nick said, making Ava smile.

"I liked the chickens and the baby cow Papa Tim has to feed from a bottle," Mia said, as if to redeem herself from being scared.

"Yeah," Lucas said. "Nana doesn't have to go to the grocery store to get eggs. She just walks outside for them."

"The chickens lay them on hay in boxes for her."

"How good of them," Nick said.

Mia nodded sagely, and Ava had all she could do not to laugh.

Her mother entered the living room. "Who's ready for that strawberry shortcake we were too full to have at supper?"

"Me, me," the twins said.

Nick patted his flat stomach. "I think I need a walk before I'll be ready. "Ava, would you give me the farm tour?"

Her heart tripped. Slow down. He probably

wants to check on the twins' day, as he does when he comes home from work at the club.

"I can do that."

"Uncle Nick, you'd better wear boots so you don't get your shoes dirty," Lucas said. "I'll bet Papa Tim will let you use his."

"I'm sure he will," her mother said.

"We wore ones that were Ms. Ava's and her brother's when they were little," Mia said, eyeing Ava's feet. "I don't think they'll fit you now. Maybe you can wear Nana Bonnie's."

"Thanks, I'll do that."

Her mother scooted the kids off to the kitchen. "Who wants to help me put the shortcakes together?"

A plot to get them alone? But hadn't Mom discouraged that earlier? Ava looked at Nick to find him looking at her. His simple glance encouraged a yearning she could do without.

"Ah, the boots are on the stairs to the basement from the outside door. Through the kitchen." She worked at keeping her steps to a casual walk. "See you later," she said to her mother and the kids as they passed them.

Ava turned the lever to the screen door, and Nick pushed it open from above her, standing so close she could feel his heat. Or was it hers? She hurried outside to the bulkhead doors.

"I'll get them," Nick said from right behind her again. He reached down and opened both sides, stood back, and laughed, looking at the set of boots on the left side of each step and around the left wall. "How many people live here?"

"Two, right now. I'm afraid Mom has kept every pair we had as kids that we didn't wear out. For small visitors and grandchildren."

The grin on Nick's face waivered. "About that. I'm not sure the twins calling them Nana and Papa is the best thing."

"Me, either, but stopping them now might not be possible."

"It's that they don't have grandparents. Constance's parents are dead. As for my mother, they aren't blood."

Pain for Nick and the twins charged through Ava. "Seriously?"

"Seriously."

"I guess, we'll just have to stay friends after you go back to Philadelphia." Ava bit her lip. She'd said that out loud.

"I'm all for that."

She flushed. "I mean ..."

"I know what you mean. But Mia and Lucas will be in Texas."

In this weekend's world of family and Nick, the kids, and her as a unit, she'd momentarily forgotten about the kids going home to Constance. "You might want to suggest to Constance that she check out Senior Corps volunteer grandparents or a similar organization."

"I can do that. But I didn't bring you outside to talk about Mia and Lucas."

Ava's pulse ticked up. Why had he?

Nick scuffed his toe against the concrete foundation of the doorway, avoiding her gaze.

He'd jumped on her blurt about staying friends. Was there more?

Her pulse was racing now. She steeled herself to give her no-brides answer to anything more. She had to. She wouldn't throw everything away on romance again.

"Um, I've never been on a working farm before. I wanted the tour. With you."

Ava gathered his last words close and strived for a light tone. "Then, what are you waiting for? Dad's boots are the ones on the top step."

"I'll forego the tractor ride," Nick said after she'd showed him the barn, equipment, and animals.

"Don't trust my driving?" Ava teased, her hand brushing his as they walked back to the house. *By accident*, she told herself.

He wrapped his hand around hers.

She *had* brushed his hand by accident, mostly, helped along by the undeniable emotion that filled her at Nick's interest and joy in seeing her world outside of New York City.

A hawk swooped down near the chicken coop, where a few of the chickens were still out. Nick stopped them to watch the hawk dip not fast enough, as the last hen scurried inside. The hawk changed course and soared back up above the trees.

"I learned something interesting about my father this morning," Nick said out of the blue. "A couple of things, actually."

"What's that?"

"He was a wildlife photographer in addition to a photojournalist. My uncle said my father had a dream of opening a wildlife preserve. Looking back, I think he may have gotten on better with animals than with people. Between my mother and him, it's a wonder I have any people skills at all."

"I think your people skills are just fine. What else did you learn?" They were close to the house, but

Ava wanted to keep him to herself talking as long as she could.

"Uncle Pete and my dad were fraternal twins. He naturally thought Mia and Lucas were mine. Sometimes I wish they were."

"Me, too. Yours, I mean. So they wouldn't be going back to Constance in a couple of weeks. I'll miss them."

Nick's eyes went soft. He leaned toward her. "And I'll ..."

They were face-to-face now, his lips close to hers. He was going to kiss her!

Instead he lifted his head. "You go in without me. I want to think about some things."

Her? No. He must have greater things to think about.

As if something outside her was controlling her actions, Ava rose on her toes and kissed Nick's cheek. "If you're sure you don't want company, I'll see you inside."

Why had she done that? So he *would* think of her. How pathetic was that? She was falling into the flirty pattern of the old Ava. She turned so he wouldn't see the blush that was probably covering all of her.

"Okay," he said in his normal tone.

I won't look back. I won't look back. I won't look back, she chimed to herself. She made it to the porch before she did. His gaze was fixed on her.

She rushed inside, her emotions ping-ponging between joy and mortification.

———

Nick woke the next morning from a dream replay of yesterday evening, except in his dream, he'd carried through his impulse to kiss Ava. And it hadn't been on the cheek. He hadn't seen Ava again last night. When he'd gone in a half hour later, her mother had said Ava had gone over to a friend's house. Nick stretched. Had his intention chased her away? But she'd kissed him, albeit on the cheek. A friendly kiss. Once the twins went back to Constance—he winced at the thought —he needed to explore with Ava where their friendship might lead.

He showered and dressed and went downstairs to find only Ava and the kids in the kitchen.

"Good morning. Mom left us a breakfast casserole this morning," Ava said as if nothing had happened between them last evening. His stomach clenched with more than the inviting aroma of the casserole. Maybe nothing had for Ava. Could be she was in the habit of kissing friends goodbye?

"Where's your mom?"

Ava handed him a plate and fork. "She and Dad have a stall at the local farmers market. A holiday weekend usually brings in a big crowd. For around here."

Nick placed the fork on the table in front of an empty chair and helped himself to breakfast and a mug of coffee.

"I wanted to go with Nana and Papa," Mia said.

Nick swallowed his mouthful of coffee. Ava's parents were just Nana and Papa now?

"They have candy and other good stuff at the farmers market near our house …"

"Our *old* house," Lucas corrected.

Ava caught his gaze and held it. This was the first the twins had said anything about Philadelphia or Constance in a couple of weeks. Were they getting homesick, missing Constance?

"You remember Uncle Nick. You used to come with us." Mia's second sentence sounded like an accusation.

"I remember."

"Mom explained to them that our market might not have quite as many things as the one they're used to and that we ... you ... are taking them to a party this afternoon. Mia thought they could do both. Go with Mom and Dad and we could pick them up from market for the party."

Nick reached over and ruffled Mia's hair. "You have all the angles, don't you?"

Mia scrunched her face. "I don't know what you mean,"

"You think of everything," he said.

"Someone has to, or we might miss something."

Mia's retort made Nick choke on his food.

Ava rushed over and patted him on his back. "You okay?"

He nodded his *yes*, although he might not be if she continued touching him. She was rubbing his back between his shoulder blades now. Nick sipped his coffee, found his voice and assured Ava he was fine.

She went back to her seat and he concentrated on eating his breakfast, thoughts about last evening interrupting his concentration. Had Ava always been demonstrative, and he hadn't noticed it before? Or had something changed for both of them last night? Or was he so nervous about being with his father's family this afternoon that in his mind, he was making Ava his life raft?

"What time do you want to leave?" she asked, followed by Lucas asking what the clock numbers would be.

"Hmm?"

She laughed, the sound rippling through him. "I'm going to have to tell Mom you liked her casserole so much you blocked out everything else in the room. "Lucas and I asked you what time we have to leave."

"Uncle Pete said to come any time after noon. We're good if we leave between 11:00 and 11:30."

"But what are the numbers?" Lucas asked. "Nana's clock is different."

"Yes, it is. It's an analog clock. The clock on my phone and the DVR are digital clocks." Nick got a kick out of the little boy's solemn nod. "Do you see the big and the little hands?"

"Yes."

"We can leave once the little hand points to the eleven and the big hand gets to the twelve."

"Got it," Lucas said.

"Should I make anything to bring?" Ava asked. "You said it was a cookout."

Nick stilled. If it were his mother giving the party, it would be catered. But he didn't get that impression from his uncle. "I don't think we're expected to bring anything, but who wouldn't want fresh strawberries. That is if there are any and your mother wouldn't mind."

Ava waved him off. "She wouldn't mind. By now she and Dad have had all the strawberries they'll want for a good while. Her patch always produces enough for a family of five, at least."

Nick finished the last of his coffee. "I've got some work I'd like to do this morning, if you could take the kids out to pick the strawberries."

"No problem. But dishes first, guys."

Nick dutifully followed the kids, clearing his place and lining up behind them by the dishwasher to hand the dishes to Ava. Their fingers brushed his as he handed her his plate, making him acutely aware of how soft her skin was. He cleared his throat and hung on to his mug.

The corners of her mouth twitched up. Were her lips always that rosy pink or was she wearing lipstick? "I'll grab the rest of the coffee and be in my room."

"I'll let you know when it's time to go to the party," Lucas said.

As if he wouldn't be counting the minutes in both anticipation and trepidation.

9

"Ms. Ava, the little hand of the clock is pointing at eleven and the big hand is past the twelve, almost to the one," Lucas said.

"So it is. Would you go let your uncle know while Mia and I finish washing the strawberries?"

"Yes, we don't want to be late for the party." Lucas scooted off.

It had taken longer than Ava had expected to pick the strawberries, since the twins had wanted to check on the "baby cows" first and had discovered a barn cat with a litter of kittens.

"All done," she said, turning off the water and shaking the colander that held the berries. "Let's pick out a pretty bowl to put them in."

"Okay," Mia said.

Ava opened the upper cupboard where her mother kept serving bowls.

"I can't see," the little girl complained.

"Up you go." Ava lifted her to the countertop.

"I like the pink one." Mia pointed to a rose-tinted crystal bowl that had belonged to Ava's grandmother.

She lifted it out of the cupboard. "I've always liked that one, too, and it will look pretty filled with strawberries."

"Pink is my favorite color. Is it yours, Ms. Ava?"

Ava thought for a moment. "No, green is, but my mother doesn't have any green bowls." She let Mia sit on the counter while she poured the berries into the bowl. They just fit.

Lucas trotted into the kitchen. "Uncle Nick said he'll be ready in a minute, and we won't be late for the party."

"Good." Ava inspected the twins. She'd washed their hands and faces when they'd come in. "I'll put plastic wrap over the bowl of strawberries, and we can go get into the car." She touched her lips. It was going to be a long ride to Nick's uncle's, and after her impulsive kiss last evening, the less face-to-face time with Nick, the better. She thanked God for the twins' presence in the car and could only hope they wouldn't fall asleep on the drive.

"Will Uncle Nick find us in the car?" Lucas asked.

"I'm sure he will." She picked up the bowl. "Who can get the door for me?"

"I can." A deep voice said behind her, startling her and almost making Ava lose her grip on the bowl.

She stepped aside to avoid Nick's arm brushing hers when he reached for the doorknob and let the kids go ahead. "Turn the inside lock, so the door will lock behind you."

"What about the deadbolt?" Nick asked.

She laughed. "This is Genesee. My parents will probably be surprised to find the door locked at all."

Ava relaxed for the drive when it became apparent the twins were more than up to keeping conversation going with their questions and observations.

"There's another golf course, Uncle Nick. Is it the right one for our turn?" Lucas asked. He'd been helping Nick with the driving directions.

"It is," Nick said, taking a left turn on the street where the directions in Ava's lap said his uncle lived.

"Now look for the number 248 on a mailbox,"

Ava added. "It's a gray colonial with pewter blue trim."

"What's a colonial?" Mia asked.

"A tall house with windows upstairs and down."

"There will probably be lots of cars in the driveway," Nick said. He looked at Ava. "Or, at least, I think so. I have three cousins who are married and have children."

"Our age?" Mia asked.

"I'm relatively sure, but I was six when I last saw my cousins, and there were only the two boys. We'll find out. And my aunt's family will be there, too, with nieces and nephews."

Ava's stomach churned. She never used to feel uncomfortable in crowds or meeting new people. Only since she'd moved to New York. With the exception of the No Brides Club members and Nick.

"2-4-8," Lucas recited from behind her. "That's the house."

"And like I said, there are lots cars in the driveway." Nick parked in front of the house and got out of the car.

Ava breathed in deeply while she watched him walk around the front of the car to let Mia and Lucas out on the side of the car facing the house. If Nick was harboring any insecurities about meeting family he hadn't seen since he was about the twins' age, he wasn't showing it. She reached down to get her purse from the floor.

"Yip." Ava almost Bumped her head on the dashboard when Nick opened the front door instead of the backseat one as she'd expected. She retightened her grip on the bowl she held so the strawberries wouldn't go flying.

"Are you okay?" Nick asked.

"Yes. I was expecting you to open the back door."

"You don't need to be nervous. I'm nervous enough for both of us."

Ava warmed at Nick's confession and laughed. "I'll try to keep that in mind."

Ava and Nick walked up the slate path to the front door, each with a twin's hand firmly in theirs.

Before Nick could press the doorbell, his uncle yelled through the open door. "Come in. You're right on time."

Nick's uncle closed the door behind them. "You must be Nick's friend, Ava."

"Yes, Ava Lewis."

"And these little people are?" He grinned at the twins.

"Mia," the little girl said.

"And Lucas." He edged closer to Ava.

"Glad to meet you. I'm Nick's Uncle Pete."

"You have an uncle, too, Uncle Nick?" Lucas asked.

"Yes, I do."

Mia eyed Nick's uncle and Nick. "You look more like a papa."

"Well, you're right, Mia. I'm a papa and an uncle."

"Can we call you Papa?" Lucas asked.

"That's what they've been calling my dad." Ava said. *Against our better judgment.*

"You most certainly can," Uncle Pete said. "That's what my other grandchildren call me."

Ava caught Nick's gaze. She'd thought he'd explained the situation to his uncle.

Nick grimaced, and Ava picked up that he had.

"Come out back and meet everyone." Uncle Pete took them through the house to the back yard and started the introductions with his grandchildren who were making use of an intricate jungle gym swing set.

"Can we play?" Mia asked.

"They'll be fine," Uncle Pete assured her and Nick, leading them back to the adults.

Nick gave his aunt Sandy a hug and a "Happy Birthday."

Ava wished her one, too. "We brought some fresh strawberries."

"How wonderful. Thank you. I'll put the strawberries on the table with the other food."

Ava's gaze followed her to the table, which looked to hold the same kind of potluck food contributions her family's get togethers usually offered. She relaxed a couple of notches.

Pete reacquainted Nick with his two cousins and introduced them to Ava. As he finished, a woman who looked to be about her age with a toddler on her hip joined them.

"And this is our youngest, Claire."

"Ah, I finally get to meet you," Nick said giving her a one-armed hug.

"Yes, and I plead the fifth on anything my father has told you about me."

Nick laughed and chucked the toddler under the chin. "And who is this little person?"

"Cole" the child shouted. "Up." He reached for Nick.

Ava took in the little boy's fine reddish hair and her family resemblance to Nick, and thought, heart swelling, *this is what Nick's own child might look like.*

Nick's uncle's voice rescued her from the dangerous place her thoughts had taken her.

"This is Nick's friend, Ava Lewis. You two girls have something in common. Claire just graduated from the University of Buffalo Law School."

"Nice to meet you. I'm starting law school at NYU in the fall." Ava couldn't help admiring that Claire had done law school with a family. "Have you found a position yet?"

"Yes, with a local foundation assisting hospitalized and other children and their families, with legal issues that impact their health and well-being."

Ava had no trouble picking up Claire's excitement about her job. "Wow. I'm double majoring in law and social work with a goal of being a child advocate. I used to be a preschool teacher."

Within minutes Ava and Claire had become fast friends, lifting the cloud that had had Ava doubting her ability to fit in at law school as she had at home and community college.

"Well, guys." Nick's uncle's voice boomed. "Let's leave the ladies to talk and go get something to drink.

"I second that," Nick's cousin Adam, who'd joined them, said.

Only half listening to Adam, Ava watched Nick walk away, feeling a pang of desertion.

"And so," Claire said, when the men were gone.

"You and Nick?" Claire made a parody of a lovesick expression.

"Just friends."

"That's what they all say," Claire teased.

No, that's what I have to say until I finish law school.

Claire smiled and hitched Cole up on her hip, her very presence mocking Ava's silent declaration.

———

Standing around the cooler with his uncle and cousins, Nick couldn't help himself from glancing over to Ava and Claire.

"Don't worry," his cousin Adam said, "she's safe with Claire. Since she's already a law student, I'm guessing she's already in league with Claire's way of independent thinking."

"Don't let Adam try to get all macho on you. His wife is an engineer, and he works for her company," Nick's other cousin Matt said.

Adam shrugged. "That's how we met. And I have to say my special benefit of being *only* the senior vice president outweighs any disadvantages." He wagged his eyebrows.

"I'm not worried. Ava and I are only friends. She

watches the twins when I'm working." Hadn't his uncle told his cousins?

"I didn't tell the rest of the family, except your aunt," Uncle Pete said. "I thought you could explain it better than I can."

Thanks, Uncle Nick. Nick explained the situation with the twins, Ava caring for them, and them all staying with Ava's parents, ending with "I know, it's kind of out there."

Claire's husband, who'd joined them, looked over his shoulder at Ava and his wife. "You sure you want to keep it at just friends?"

No. He wasn't sure at all that that's where he wanted to keep it, but he needed to respect Ava's wishes. Nick found himself rubbing the knuckles of his right hand against his left palm and stopped himself. He looked up to see the guy grinning, his gaze on Nick's still clenched fist.

"I guess I got my answer," Claire's husband said.

"Cool it, boys," Uncle Pete said, "while I go relieve my brother-in-law on the grill."

Nick dropped his hands to his sides, embarrassed and surprised at the strength of the feelings Claire's husband's comment had brought out in him.

The conversation turned to the slightly more benign upcoming NFL preseason schedule. Most of the guys were stalwart support-them-whatever Buffalo Bills fans, while Nick was a Philadelphia Eagles supporter, and Aunt Sandy's nephew, who'd also joined them, was New England Patriots fan.

Nick felt a tug on his jeans pantleg.

"Uncle Nick," Lucas said, "Uncle Papa said we can eat now. I was helping him cook hot dogs and hamburgers."

Struggling to keep a straight face at the Uncle Papa, Nick glanced at the jungle gym where he and Ava had left the kids. Most of them looked to still be there. "Did you get tired of the jungle gym?" he probed to see if there had been some kind of problem that prompted Lucas to leave the group.

"Yeah, it was mostly girls and babies. The bigger guys were helping Uncle Papa."

"I see." While Nick knew it would surface sometime, Lucas's distain for playing only with girls was new to him. The twins were growing up. Sadness settled over him. And he would miss seeing most of it.

He shook off his thoughts. Today he'd make the most of being with them. And with Ava. "We'd better go find Ms. Ava. We don't want her to miss out on the food."

"No," Lucas agreed. "Maybe we better look for Mia, too."

He took Lucas's hand and scanned the yard, finding Ava sitting in a lawn chair under the shade trees lining the back of the yard with Claire and his aunt. Cole was curled up on Ava's lap, looking to be fast asleep. Seeing Ava with Cole tugged at his heart strings in a way he'd never felt before.

"I've found Ms. Ava." Nick cleared the hoarseness from his voice. "Let's tell her and, then, all look for Mia." His insides went soft again at the four of them as a unit. They were for today. Or, at least he could pretend they were.

As he and Lucas got closer, Ava waved to them.

Lucas ran over shouting "Uncle Papa says it's time to eat."

When Nick caught up, Ava was handing the sleeping toddler to Claire, her expression that of the Madonna on a Christmas card. She smiled some of that radiance at him. "Your aunt was telling me that Cole looks just like you did at that age."

Nick wanted to think part of the expression that had been on Ava's face was due to what his aunt had said. That she'd thought as he had that Cole was what a child of his might look like. He rubbed the back of his neck. He must have been out in the direct sun too long.

"We don't want to miss the food," Ava said. "Especially, Aunt Sandy, since it's her party."

Lucas positioned himself in front of Aunt Sandy, feet apart. "Are you Uncle Papa's Nana?"

His aunt looked at Nick with a questioning expression. He explained. "And when Uncle Pete said he was both an uncle and a Papa, Lucas put the two together."

"I see. No Lucas, I'm not Nana."

Lucas's smile dimmed.

Nick's heart dropped. That wasn't like the Aunt Sandy he'd known as a child. But wasn't it what he'd wanted? To discourage Ava's parents and his uncle and aunt from encouraging the kids from thinking of them as grandparents.

"I'm married to Uncle Papa. All my grandchildren call me Grammy. So you can call me Aunt Grammy, if you like."

The corners of Lucas's mouth popped back up. "I'll tell Mia when we find her."

Nick caught Ava's gaze with his. She shrugged palms up. Right. What could they do? And it was only for one day.

Mia skipped over to them as they started toward the long table set along one side of the yard.

"Mia," Lucas called pointing at Aunt Sandy. "This is Uncle Papa's Nana, but she likes to be called Grammy."

"She's not Uncle Papa's Nana." Mia put on her mantle of superiority. "She's his wife and everyone else's grandmother. That's why she's called Grammy. Right Uncle Nick?"

He gave up. "Something like that. But you could have told your brother in a nicer way."

Mia looked contrite for a moment before asking Claire, "Who are you?"

"I'm your uncle's cousin Claire, and this is Cole."

Seemingly satisfied, Mia challenged her brother. "Race you to the table."

"Uncle Nick, I'll save you and Ms. Ava a seat," Lucas shouted back to them as he took off after Mia.

Claire laughed. "However, did you two do it when they were Cole's age? He alone wears my husband and me out." She clapped her fingertips over her mouth. "I'm sorry. I forgot. You four have such a great family dynamic."

"Thanks. I think." Nick took his cousin's words as a compliment, albeit a sad one. He couldn't remember his mother, father, and him acting together as anything. It was more his parents pitting themselves against each other, or his mother directing his father to take him somewhere. Now, that he thought about it, the three of them rarely went anywhere together.

"A lot of credit goes to Nick." Ava said. "He's so good with them."

Nick blew on his fingernails and polished them on his shirt front to cover up how much Ava's praise had gotten to him.

"I'm afraid we've created a monster," Claire said.

Ava looked him over, eyes twinkling. "Monster or no, he knows where the food is, and I'm starved." She looped her arm through his.

Nick offered his other arm to his cousin. To ward off some of the pleasure rolling through him from Ava close beside him? Touching him. To get control of himself?

"No thanks. I need both arms for my little man. But lead away."

So he'd cede to the pleasure, give up his control. The fragrance that he'd come to think of as Ava's scent drifted toward him. *Self-control could be overrated.*

"Uncle Nick, Ms. Ava. We saved seats for you,"

Mia said from a folding chair at the table, when they got close.

His moment of quiet closeness was over.

Ava pulled her arm from his, affirming so.

"See." Mia pointed. "The flat napkins mean the seat is saved. The lady told me."

Nick didn't know who Mia meant. No one was near them now. But he saw other places at the table where the napkins had been unrolled and laid flat.

"Good job," Ava said.

"Thank you," he mouthed before facing the twins. "Let's get in line and get our food before it's all gone."

Mia and Lucas scrambled down and stayed next to him and Ava in the line. Seated at the table not long afterwards with Lucas to his left, Ava and Mia to the right, and family all around them, Nick allowed his feeling of belonging to resurface. It was a beautiful summer day, with great food, people he cared about.

And nothing to spoil it.

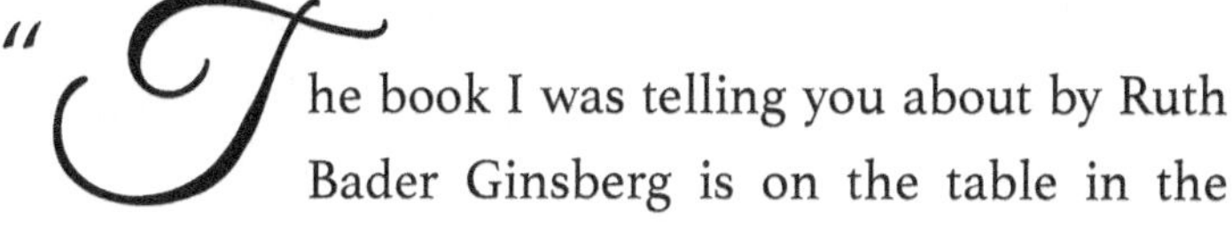

"The book I was telling you about by Ruth Bader Ginsberg is on the table in the living room," Claire said. "Go ahead and get it while I change Cole upstairs."

Ava welcomed the chance to have a more leisurely look at the house than she'd gotten when Nick's uncle had ushered them through to the back door. She was sure the furniture and decorations were much more expensive than the ones her parents had, but the rooms had the same family-used welcoming feeling.

She found the book right off, picked it up, and leafed through it. Ava couldn't wait to read it but might have to make that a treat for after she'd finished her daily course assignments.

A buzz at the front door made her close the book. "I'll get it," she shouted up to Claire.

"Thanks."

The doorbell buzzed again. *Okay, I'm coming.*

Ava opened the door to a tall reed-thin woman with light brown hair pulled back into what Ava assumed was a French twist. Her tailored capris and "casual" blouse, along with understated perfectly coordinated jewelry shouted money.

"Is this the Jansen residence?" the woman asked.

"Yes. You must be here for the birthday party. Come in." Ava smiled a welcome that wasn't returned.

The woman stepped inside and looked around the room with an expression that bordered on distaste. "And you must be Peter's youngest."

"No, Claire is upstairs changing the baby."

"Oh, there are children here?"

It was a family party. What did the woman expect? "Yes, and I'm Ava Lewis, a friend of the Jansen's nephew."

Ava shifted her weight from left to right under the woman's slow inscrutable once over. Her stomach clenched. The woman had to be ...

"I'm Kathryn Jansen."

Nick's mother.

"And I assume you're referring to Nicholas."

"Yes, let me show you outside to the party."

"Outdoors. How typical of Peter."

Ava didn't know if the woman was speaking to her or to herself. Either way it grated on her nerves. "Yes, it's a potluck barbeque," she said brightly, stretching things a bit, since at least part of the refreshments had been catered. Ava shouldn't have, but she reveled in Kathryn's sour expression.

She escorted the older woman to the back deck and called out, "Look who's here," earning her a look darker than she'd imagined.

Uncle Pete strode over and up the deck steps.

"Kathryn. You came just in time for cake. You're looking well."

"Yes. I was at the Shakespeare Festival in Ontario. It ended yesterday, so I rented a car and drove down. Where's Nicholas?" Nick's mother looked off over the yard.

"Last I saw him, he was playing tag with the kids in the far back."

"I see." Nick's mother brushed by his uncle and down the steps."

"Shall we?" Pete said. He and Ava walked together down the steps and into the yard.

"Poor Nick," she said to herself.

"You've got that right," his uncle said.

Or maybe not to herself.

"Kathy doesn't seem to have changed in twenty-five years." He glanced around them. "Except I suspect the hair color may not be her own anymore," he said with a conspiratorial grin. "And don't call her Kathy. It'll set her off."

"I'm playing it safe and calling her Mrs. Jansen, if anything."

"Make that Ms. Jansen, and you may escape the day unscathed, unlike our poor Nick."

Ms. Jansen stopped at the food table where

Nick's Aunt Sandy was cutting her birthday cake, shook her head, and handed Sandy a small gift.

"That would be earrings for pierced ears. Sandy doesn't have pierced ears. Never has and Kathy knows it. But that's what she's given Sandy every birthday and Christmas we were in contact."

"Odd," was all Ava could say.

"In the past, Sandy has donated the earrings to charities to be auctioned off."

Ava couldn't help laughing. "Good for her. I'd better go get the kids for cake. I'm sure Nick's mother will want to talk with him in private." The thought of Nick's mother having a private conversation with him hung like a razor-sharp blade above her as she strode across the lawn, arriving at the group to hear Nick say in an emotionless tone, "Mother. What a surprise."

Ava was sure it was that and more. "I'll take the kids to get cake."

"Thanks," Nick said. "Mother, this is a friend ..."

His mother cut him off. "We've met."

Mia appeared by Ava's side. "We haven't," the little girl said.

"If you're Uncle Nick's mother, are you a Nana or a Grammy?" Lucas asked.

Ms. Jansen's eyes widen in what Ava could read only as horror.

"Ms. Ava's mother is a Nana, but Uncle Nick's aunt is a Grammy," Lucas explained.

"I'm neither," Nick's mother said sharply.

"Oh," Lucas said, looking confused.

"Come on guys. Let's get cake," Ava said. "You know where I'll be if you need me."

"Thanks." Nick nodded, his eyes saying much more than his word.

Ava hustled the kids to the table for cake, humming to herself. She liked being there, wanted to be there for Nick. Not just for the kids. And a warm feeling she hadn't experienced before said that unlike her ex-fiancé, Nick would be there for her, too, if she needed him.

10

"Her children?" his mother asked when he turned to her from watching Ava leave.

Incredulous. His mother didn't remember Mia and Lucas. He searched her face or was pretending not to.

"She looks awfully young to have children that old."

"Mother, they aren't Ava's. They're Constance's niece and nephew."

"I remember, the children foisted on her by Social Services."

He wasn't going to correct her. Constance had willingly taken the twins.

"What are they doing here with you? Or is Constance here, too." His mother's tone brightened.

"They're with me because Constance is on a honeymoon cruise with her husband. Her mother couldn't take them, so she asked me. His mother had no need to know the whole story.

His mother shook her head. "You should have never let her get away. She was charming and polished, the perfect complement to you and your career. When you still had a career. She knew how to entertain, help you up the corporate ladder."

But he'd gone as far up the corporate ladder at his old job as he'd wanted to. And he and Constance had mutually agreed to split. She liked being connected to a corporate executive with all the perks that come with that position. She didn't have any desire to spend her life with a struggling sm all business owner. And it had hurt, but Constance hadn't had faith in him to move beyond struggling.

"But you didn't come to talk about Constance and the twins. Nor, I suspect, did you come to celebrate Aunt Sandy's birthday with family."

"You're right there. Can we go somewhere private to talk, preferably out of the sun."

"We can go inside. I don't think anyone else is in there." He escorted his mother toward the house.

"Uncle Nick," Lucas called as they passed the table with the cake.

His mother winced and murmured, "You shouldn't let them call you that."

"Aunt Grammy has chocolate and `nilla birthday cake. I got both."

"And I got a big piece of chocolate because I like it best," Mia said.

The twins' frosting-framed grins pushed away most of the dread that had wormed its way into him at the prospect of one of his mother's *talks*.

Ava joined them napkins in hand and wiped Lucas and Mia's faces. "I'll bet Uncle Nick could have guessed what kind of cake you guys were eating from the crumbs and frosting on your faces."

"Even me, with two kinds?" Luca asked.

"Even you." Ava tapped him on the tip of his nose, making Nick's heart swell with how good she was with the kids. And with him.

"That's it. She's your nanny. You brought her to take care of the children. Why didn't you say so?" his mother said.

"Ava. Is. Not. My. Nanny," he gritted out. "She's a close friend and a law student who lives in the apartment complex where I'm staying in New York. Her parents live on the way here, so I invited her along for company on the drive and so she could visit with her parents. That's where we're staying. Her parents have a farm near Genesee."

He'd told her more than he'd needed to, but it was worth the smile and soft look he received from Ava.

"Yeah," Lucas piped up. "A farm with cows and chickens and `quipment and everything."

Beside him, Mia dropped her gaze to Nick's mother's wedge sandals and warned, "If you come to visit and want to see the cows, you have to borrow Nana's rubber boots, so you don't get your shoes all icky."

"Nicholas, our talk," his mother said, her face colored with disdain.

"Go inside. I'll be right there."

His mother walked away.

"This shouldn't take long," he said.

"Good luck," Ava said.

Nick pretended to catch her words in his hand. "Got it." He pressed his hand to his chest."

"What are you doing?" Mia asked.

"Catching Ms. Ava's 'good luck' to take with me."

"Take ours, too," the little girl said. "Good luck."

"Good luck," her brother echoed.

Nick grabbed the air with one hand and then the

other, made as if he were making a snowball, and clapped his right hand to his chest.

The twins giggled.

One more glance at Ava's beautiful smile and he had the armor he needed to deal with his mother. He took his mother inside to the living room. "So what's this about?"

"I got Peter's invitation and had planned to be up in Ontario for the Shakespeare festival this week, so I thought it would give me a good opportunity to catch you here and talk in person."

Nick motioned her to the couch. It wasn't like Mother to make small talk and not get right to the point. Once she was seated, he sat in a chair facing her.

"This trip. Does it mean you're finishing the work for Peter?"

"I should be done soon, except for my seat on Uncle Pete's nonprofit board. That advising is ongoing."

His mother pressed her lips in a thin line before speaking. "I have a business opportunity for you."

Nick's tensed muscles relaxed some. His mother had a lot of business contacts in Philadelphia, and he didn't have anything solid lined up yet for after he finished his work for Uncle Pete. He leaned forward.

"It's in mergers and acquisitions. The corporation isn't as big as the one you were with before."

"Mother." He dropped back against the chair back. "I have my own company. I'm not looking for a position with someone else."

She raised her hand. "Hear me out."

"Fine." The discussion would go quicker if he didn't interrupt.

"As I said, it's a smaller corporation, but you'd have greater opportunity to advance, and the benefit package is better than what you had and far superior, I'm sure, than what you're giving yourself. I took the liberty of telling my contact that you'd be calling. I'll email you the details."

"Thanks for thinking of me. But no thanks."

"You haven't even seen the details," his mother protested.

"Nor do I want to. I'm happy doing what I'm doing."

She just stared at him, giving Nick the sad feeling that his mother had no idea how it felt to be happy with your work, your life.

"That attitude lost you Constance and won't help you attract another woman of her caliber. You're past thirty. It's time you were settled.

As if he didn't know how old he was or would

want a relationship with another woman like Constance. "No, Mother, I didn't, as you said, 'lose Constance'. We mutually agreed that we couldn't give each other what we wanted."

She stood. "I give up. Pass my goodbye on to Sandra. I'm going to my hotel."

"Mother, I'm sorry you're disappointed, but I can't live my life for you anymore than I could for Constance."

"Harrumph." His mother turned her cheek to him.

Nick walked her to the door and gave her a peck on the cheek. "Goodbye."

"Goodbye. Let me know when you're back in Philadelphia." She turned and walked out, leaving Nick in a wake of sadness.

The truth he'd learned the hard way with his mother and Constance was that people couldn't live their lives strictly to make another person happy. That didn't make anyone happy. To be truly happy, you needed to share your life as it was *with* someone else.

And all this wisdom only made for questions. Could he share his life—what you see is what you get—with Ava? And she with him?

There was only one way to find out.

"**Y**ou okay?" Ava met him on the deck when he came back out.

"Fine."

She knew he wasn't and that he wasn't ready to talk about it yet. Maybe later. She slipped her hand in his and held her breath until he squeezed it. Ava squeezed his back. "The kids are in the back playing with the others. Your aunt is with them."

"You don't mind if we leave, do you?"

"Had enough family?"

Nick frowned. She shouldn't have teased him.

"Something like that."

"Take my word for it, even in close families, sometimes you need breathing room."

"Uncle Nick," Mia called as soon as they were in shouting distance. "Watch. I learned to do a cartwheel." The little girl promptly demonstrated.

Ava and Nick clapped. "Nice."

"And I learned to stand on my head," Lucas said, waiting until they got close before he showed them and stayed up long enough for them to clap and praise him.

"Adam's girls take gymnastics, and they were

holding court showing what they can do and teaching the others," Nick's aunt explained.

"Can you do a cartwheel or stand on your head Uncle Nick?" Lucas asked.

"I used to be able to stand on my head, but I never mastered cartwheels."

"I could do both," Ava boasted. "I was a cheerleader when I was in high school."

"Why am I not surprised," Nick quipped, his mood improved by the twins' antics.

"Show us," Mia demanded.

"Yes, show us," Nick challenged her.

"I don't know about the headstand but watch this." Ava sucked in a breath, ran a few steps, and executed a perfect cartwheel.

"Show off," Nick said.

"Huh! Put your money where your mouth is," Ava shot back.

"Okay, you asked." Nick raised his arms and folded his hands behind his head, flexing his biceps and chest muscles and keeping Ava's attention riveted. Then, he shook out his hands and legs and stilled, eyes closed.

Ava took the opportunity to enjoy the view, jerking her gaze away when he opened his eyes.

"Here's something for you to watch." Nick took

off at twice the speed of Ava and went into a front flip, followed immediately by a back flip.

He sauntered back to "Wow, Uncle Nick," from the twins.

"You're going to have to show me how to do that," Ava said.

"Me too." "Yeah," the kids said.

"I'll think about it if I'm still walking tomorrow." Nick laughed.

"I'll help you, old man." Ava lifted his left hand and draped it across her shoulders. "Lean on me."

Nick smiled down at her, and with a start, Ava realized her offer stood in more ways than the physical one.

"Aunt Sandy," he said, we should get going. "I'm so glad we've reconnected. I've really enjoyed myself today." Nick lifted his arm off Ava's shoulder to hug his aunt goodbye.

Ava felt as if he'd taken something precious from her.

"I hope that means we'll be seeing more of all of you," Aunt Sandy said, hugging the twins and Ava.

Over his aunt's shoulder, Ava saw Nick's smile fade and the glimpse of joy in his eyes Ava had seen when she'd called him old man disappear.

"And you'll have to come with Uncle Pete the

next time he comes to New York and see us." Nick looked as if he were going to say more, but he didn't. All too soon for Ava, he'd be back in Philadelphia.

"I will," his aunt said. "Make sure you get your cake to take back with you, Mia and Lucas."

"We will."

Nick draped his arms around Ava's shoulders again and they said their goodbyes to everyone else on their way to the house, with a stop at the cake table. Someone had sliced up the rest of the cake and put it in individual-sized to-go containers.

"I think we better take some for Nana and Papa," Mia said.

Ava nodded yes. "I'm sure they'd love some."

"What kind do they like?" Lucas asked.

"They'll like any kind you choose for them. But why not get them one chocolate and one vanilla. They can always share," Ava answered.

"Good thinking, Ms. Ava."

When she and Nick finally ushered the twins out the front door to the car, a pang twisted Ava's insides. She didn't want the day to be over. It had been fun being a foursome with Nick's family.

"You, too?" Nick asked as if he could read her thoughts, which might not be a good thing.

"I hate to leave."

"Same here."

They each buckled one twin in in silence, and the kids talked enough on the drive to her parents' that Nick and Ava didn't have to and break the bubble they'd left Pete and Sandy's in.

Her mother was waiting for them on the porch when they drove up, and Mia and Lucas took off like little rockets as soon as Ava and Nick unbuckled their seatbelts.

Both were in her mother's embrace talking away when Ava and Nick trudged up the porch stairs with the luggage.

"You both look tired," her mother said. "Why don't we all go in and get a cold drink. Then you and Nick can come out here and wind down, enjoy the beautiful summer evening. I'm sure Mia and Lucas won't mind me giving them their baths and getting them ready for you know what."

"I know what," Mia.

"What?" Ava's mother rubbed noses with the little girl, who answered, "Bed," with a face that made the adults laugh.

"Yes, you need to rest up for your trip home tomorrow."

Ava's mother's reference to home gave Ava a bittersweet lump in her throat. Would the foursome-bond she'd felt at Nick's aunt and uncle's travel back with them? Should she even try to make it last? They'd only be together until the twins and Nick went back to their real homes. To Texas. And Philadelphia.

"A cold drink and a wind down sound good to me." Nick broke into her moment of contemplation.

"Me also," she said.

He held the door open for them. "Ladies first."

"We go last because we're the gentlemen, right Uncle Nick," Lucas said, earning another laugh from the adults.

"Right, buddy." Nick's expression softened as he smiled at Lucas, then her as she brushed past him inside,

Her heart warmed. Maybe it would be okay to pretend they were a foursome, to not think about Nick and the twins leaving. Just for the rest of their time here.

———

Ava was already sitting on the porch swing to one side. An invitation to join her on the other instead of sitting in one of the Adirondack chairs? He wasn't going to wait for any more invitation in case there wasn't one.

"Get lost?" she teased.

He sat on the swing, his shoulder to hers and looked down. She was so beautiful, even when she looked tired. "I got sidelined by your father who wanted to know if I used his short-cut for the drive to Uncle Pete's and how it worked out."

Ava sipped her iced tea. "That's Dad." Her hip touched his.

Had she moved closer, or had he? No matter. She wasn't moving back away.

"I had a really good time today with your family."

"I did, too."

"Even with your mother's surprise drop-in?"

"Even with that." He stretched his arm along the back of the swing behind her.

"Do you want to talk about it?"

"Not really."

"It might help. I'm a good listener and we don't have any mutual friends I can talk behind your back with."

"Who could turn down a recommendation like that?"

She leaned her head on his shoulder and he

couldn't help but wonder if she'd felt the jolt of heated surprise that ran through him. "I'm serious," she said softly.

"I am, too."

"So, talk. Obviously, your mother wasn't there for your aunt's birthday. She barely spoke with her."

"No, she'd been up in Ontario at a Shakespeare festival and deigned to come to the party long enough to tell me about a business opportunity before flying out of Buffalo back to Philadelphia."

"And that's a bad thing."

"No." He released a breath through his nose. "It could have been a good thing, if it had actually been an opportunity for my company. But it was a job opening at a corporation one of her business contacts owns. In mergers and acquisitions." He dropped his arm to her shoulder. "From there it devolved into the usual tangent on the foolishness of going into business for myself, how I'll never succeed."

"I can sympathize with that tone of never hitting the right key. Being the youngest in my family by far, I've always been protected by all of them, never pushed to try my wings."

To Nick that sounded almost the opposite of his upbringing. How could Ava sympathize? He parted his lips, but before he could speak, Ava pressed her forefinger to his lips, and he fought a wild urge to touch his tongue to it.

"Let me finish. When I planned only to get my associate's degree, they did press me to go on for my bachelor's. But after I broke my engagement …"

Ava hadn't mentioned a broken engagement before. Something more they had in common. He opened himself more to her.

"When I decided to finish the almost two-years of college classes I needed for my bachelor's degree online in a year, none of them thought I could do it."

"But you did, didn't you?" Ava's smile in reply lit his heart like a blow torch.

"And I don't think any of them feel I'm cut out to be an attorney. I think that's part of Kate's reason for hooking me up with her No Brides Club. To show me the reality of a totally career-focused life, even for only a period of time. Your cousin, Claire, showed me another side of that."

"I'm glad. It really is a matter of balance—a balance of work and being there for your partner. I couldn't find it with Constance or with my former job." Nick laughed, thinking back to his mother's next gripe. "Mother's grand finale was a new lecture point on how my going into business for myself was no way to attract a socially upward wife to help me achieve real financial success. She reminded me I wasn't getting any younger."

Ava stiffened.

What had possessed him to add the wife and age parts? Ava had seemed more than fine with his arm around her until then. He needed a save. "She already warned me about you."

She relaxed as quickly as she'd tensed. "Me." The surprise in her voice dragged the word out.

"Until she decided you were the nanny. Then, I apparently was safe."

Ava's giggle waved over him, washing away the bitterness that had taken seed talking about his mother. Talking with Constance or anyone else had never had that effect on him.

"I'm sorry, but I was having trouble with my being man-danger."

His heart thumped. She had no idea what a man-danger she was. "Never fear. I set her straight when I said you're not the nanny, but a friend, a *close* friend."

Her eyes widened at his reminder of what he'd said at the cake table. In them he read more than surprise. But he'd read women wrong before. Lots of times.

"Yeah," her voice was soft. "So that's what we are?"

"It's what I'd like us to be, what I think we are. Let's see." He turned on the swing, tipped her chin up with his finger and lowered his lips, kissing her softly at first, until she responded and then firmly, needing to release, share the emotions welling up inside him. He broke the kiss when it made him want more.

"I guess that answers that." The vibration of Ava's words against his still close lips, made him lean in for a final peck before sitting back in the swing.

"That is does."

"I have one more question."

"Shoot." He set the swing into gentle motion.

"How old are you."

That was it? "I'm thirty."

"You're younger than both Kate and my brother."

"Is that good? Does it help me meet some kind of criteria?"

She looked him full in the face. "Oh, you meet all kinds of criteria that I shouldn't even have established. But maybe we ought to test again."

He lowered his head, seeing only the yearning in her eyes. Who was he to turn down a lady's polite request, especially when that lady was Ava?

11

Nick listened to Mia and Lucas squabbling in the living room and pushed away from his desk in the bedroom. They stopped, but his concentration was broken. He stood and stretched and checked the clock on his phone. It was only 10:30. Ava wouldn't be there for at least a couple more hours. They'd fallen back into their routine of her coming to his apartment after her class to watch the kids and him leaving to work at the club office. On both Monday and Tuesday, she'd left as soon as he'd returned, saying that her course homework seemed to be growing exponentially in time and difficulty the closer she got to the end of the program. They'd had no time together, making the weekend seem like a dream, a one-time magical aberration where he and Ava belonged together.

A knock sounded on the door, followed by Lucas's, "Uncle Nick is that Ms. Ava. It's not one-three-O."

"Let's see." Nick couldn't think who it could be besides Ava. He strode into the living room. The building superintendent more likely would have called before coming up. He looked through the peephole, clicked open the deadbolt, and reached for the doorknob. "It's Mrs. Murphy."

"Does she have her dog?" Mia asked.

"Not today." He opened the door. "Hi, Ellen. Come in."

"Hi, Mrs. Murphy," the twins said.

"Hello. You two are just the people I'm looking for," the older woman smiled broadly. "My grandchildren who are four and six are visiting. I wondered if you'd like to come see a puppet show at the library with us. If it's okay with your uncle. It starts at one."

"Can we Uncle Nick?" Mia asked.

Nick hated to disappoint the kids or question his neighbor's ability. But the twins by themselves were a handful. Adding another four- and six-year-old, seemed like way too much for one person. "Sorry, guys, Ms. Ava will be here too late to take you with Mrs. Murphy, and I really have to work."

"I don't need Ava to come," Ellen assured him.

Nick took a deep breath. "I think your taking all four children by yourself is too much." There, he'd said it.

Ellen laughed. "It certainly is. My daughter is here with my grandchildren."

"Well, in that case. They're yours for the afternoon."

"Does that mean we can go?" Lucas asked.

Nick ruffled the little boy's hair. "Yes, it does."

"And my invitation extends to coming over now to play," Ellen said.

He smiled at the generous offer. "It's up to Mia and Lucas. Do you want to go with Mrs. Murphy now?"

"Yes."

"Yes."

"Okay. Promise to behave for her and her daughter."

The twins promised.

Nick reached in his pocket for his wallet and pulled out a bill."

Ellen shook her head. "My treat. The puppet show is free, and we'll just get some ice cream on the way back."

"What time will you be back?"

"3:30, 4:00."

"Great. Thanks you so much for doing this. Have a good time." Nick squatted and hugged Mia and Lucas.

Ellen took each of the twins by the hand, and he opened the door and watched them walk down the hall to his neighbor's apartment.

He went back to work at his desk and an idea took hold. If he could get enough done in the rest of the morning, he and Ava would both be free to do something together that afternoon. He could test out sharing time with Ava without the kids and see if the attraction was as strong as what he'd felt during their weekend away. Nick went to work, putting himself so deep into it, he almost didn't hear the knock on the door several hours later.

Ava was here. He glanced at his computer screen. And he'd finished all he'd wanted to do this morning and most of what he'd planned to work on this afternoon at the club.

Another knock sounded, and he raced to the door, like one of the kids. Before he opened the door, he stilled his excitement and struck a casual pose.

"Sorry, I'm few minutes late. The professor went over."

"No problem." He closed the door and watched Ava look around the room, then toward the bedroom. "Don't tell me Mia and Lucas are napping."

"They aren't. Ellen Murphy's grandchildren and daughter are visiting, and they all went to a puppet show at the library. They won't be back until 3:30 or 4:00."

"I have my afternoon free?"

Her question made his stomach plummet with disappointment. Ava had spoken with such glee that all he could think was that she had a lot of course-work to do today and welcomed the extra free hours.

"How about you?" she asked.

"How about me, what?" He must have missed something.

"What's your afternoon look like? If you're not too busy, maybe we could do some sightseeing. I've lived here more than a month, and I haven't seen anything but the Statue of Liberty and Times Square. Not counting the kid places I've taken Mia and Lucas."

"You're in luck. I had the same idea. I made good use of my time this morning and just so happen to have my afternoon free, too. The weather's nice. How about a—*romantic*—stroll through Central Park?"

"Mmm." Ava pressed her lips together. "I grew up in nature. Nature's less romantic than you might think. Let's save that one for a time we can take the twins. If we have time before the kids get back, I'd like to see Ground Zero. It will just take me two minutes to run to my apartment and drop off my school things."

Ground Zero wasn't particularly romantic either. "With the tour, we'd be cutting it close to when the kids come back."

Disappointment flickered in Ava's eyes.

"I have an idea. While you're dropping off your stuff, I'll text Ellen and see if she'll keep Mia and Lucas a little longer and meet us at the Italian restaurant next door at 5:00 for dinner. My treat. I'll order us tour tickets, too."

Ava hiked her book bag strap up on her shoulder and surprised him with a quick hug that was over before he could physically act.

"Thanks, it's something I didn't want to see by myself." She opened the door and slipped out.

Nick watched the door close behind her before whistling his way into the bedroom to get his phone.

So far, he was scoring A-plus on his self-administered test.

———

Ava dropped her bag on the couch. She wasn't sure what had gotten into her, hugging Nick like that. She strode into her bedroom, her reflection in the mirror confronting her. What had gotten into her was the warm feelings she'd brought back with her from the weekend in Western New York. As sweet as things had been between them in Genesee, here in New York everything was all business again. He hadn't asked her to stay and eat with them Monday or Tuesday. Of course, she had told him how much coursework she had to do.

Her reflection didn't have any more answers than she did. Ava quickly changed out of the t-shirt she had on and into a dressier summer top and exchanged her sandals for athletic shoes better suited for walking. She tried to pass by the bathroom without popping in to touch-up her make-up and fluff her hair but was unsuccessful. If Nick noticed, which was doubtful, he wouldn't necessarily think she'd done the touch-up for him. Right?

Nick answered his apartment door at the first touch of her knock, as if he had been standing there waiting. Her toes tingled. Was he looking forward to their time together as much as she was?

"Hi." He joined her in the hall.

She took in the well-fitted polo shirt and khakis he'd changed into from the jeans and t-shirt he'd had on minutes ago and warmth blossomed in her chest behind her ribs. Nick had dressed for her, too. He walked her down to the complex exit on Murray Street. "I thought we'd take the Hudson River Green-way. It's a couple more minutes longer but a nicer walk."

"How far is it?"

He opened the door and held if for her. "About ten minutes."

They walked in companionable silence to West Street and crossed over to the Greenway, the sounds of the city playing around them like background music.

Nick broke the silence. "I've been wondering if you chose Ground Zero for any particular reason."

"I did." Ava collected herself. "My aunt was a flight attendant on Flight 77. Mom's sister." She swallowed the lump that had formed in her throat. "I was only five, but I remember her well."

Nick took her hand in his and squeezed.

"It's on the South Pool. Kate, my sister, took pictures for Mom when Kate moved to New York for college." She sniffled. "I want to touch my aunt's name."

He caressed her hand with his thumb. "After my upbringing, it's new to me, but I'm starting to understand how much family means to you. How much family in general can mean."

"You mean something to me, too." *There.* She'd said it.

Nick stopped walking and gazed down at her, his eyes soft, but expression unreadable. Maybe he just felt sorry for her because he didn't feel the same. She straightened. She was an adult. She had a fulfilling future ahead of her.

He brushed his lips butterfly-soft against hers. "You have no idea how much you're starting to mean to me."

Ava's knees went week. She was prepared for a rebuff, but those sweet words left her defenseless. "You know I can't put my full self into a relationship right now. I won't lose my goal and myself."

He held her gaze. "I don't want you to lose either.

Ever. Your three years of law school isn't very long compared to what I want."

"What?" The word escaped her thoughts in a whisper.

He hugged and released her. "That's not important this minute."

Relief from Nick's intensity flowed through her. She wasn't ready to be too serious yet.

"For now, we only need to explore where our relationship might go. All right?"

"Yes, I can do that." *Gladly.*

A woman walked by then with a toddler in a stroller. "I hope the twins are behaving for Ellen," Ava said to change the subject.

"Uh, uh," Nick said. "No kids. This is our time. But I hope they are, too."

"Gotcha." But Ava couldn't help thinking about how much Mia and Lucas were a part of her relationship with Nick. Would they be able to go forward after the kids went back to Constance? Or, were they too much of the glue binding her to Nick?

As if to lighten her thoughts, Nick took her hand again and swung it back and forth as they walked the rest of the Greenway and lined up at the memorial to check in for their tour. The tour flew by leaving Ava uplifted and filled with compassion for the victims, the emergency responders, and their families.

"You okay?" Nick asked.

"Very okay."

He nodded. "I've been here several times and been moved each time."

"Let's go back to the South Pool and look for my aunt's name." Nick fell in step with her. But he didn't take her hand, seeming to sense she needed space right now, which sent a ripple through her. She was both charmed by and a little wary of what she perceived as his sensitivity. He continued to hold his distance when they reached the pool.

Ava stepped closer and ran her gaze over the inscriptions until she found her aunt's name. She leaned closer and ran her finger over it and touched her finger to her lips before running it over the inscription again and straightening. Nick rested his hands on her shoulders and squeezed them when she released a sob. She didn't know how long they stood like that until she'd composed herself to face the world again.

When she turned around, she saw only Nick's soft gaze focused on her, keeping the rest of the world at bay at little longer.

va's expression when she'd turned to him almost brought Nick to his knees. If it were up to him, he'd protect her from any sadness and hurt in her life. But not only was that impossible, it would probably send her running, screaming from him. He cared for her deeply, but whatever was growing between them was so new, and he had no idea yet how strongly Ava might care for him.

"I'm hungry," he said, seeking an ice breaker.

Ava's expression froze, rather than melting. Then, she laughed, the sound chasing out his feeling of idiocy about his unrelated blurt.

"In my experience, guys are always hungry."

He draped his arm around her shoulder, and she slipped hers around his waist.

"I see," he said, aiming for a sage tone. "Then, am I to suppose you aren't hungry and wouldn't be interested in a soft-serve ice cream cone on our way back?"

"I didn't say that. I was simply making an obser-vation. Before I take you up on your offer, I want to thank you."

Nick scuffed his toe on the path. "I wanted to spend time with you."

"But you did so much more." Her voice caught, catching his heart with it. "I can't explain it. You didn't just spend time with me. You were *right* with me."

"Just being a friend." If Ava didn't let up, he was going to be nothing but a puddle at her feet.

"If that's the case, you're exactly the friend I need, mister. So friend, how did you know I love soft-serve ice cream?"

"I have my ways," he said in a comic villain voice, "and Lucas has reported how many times you've stopped for soft-serve ice cream on your afternoon outings."

"Well, in that case, let me show you which street vendor the kids and I have decided has the best ice cream."

Ava led them somewhat out of their way home to catch the ice cream vendor. "What do you think?" she asked after insisting the ice cream was her treat.

"Good."

"Just good? It's fantastic. Take my word. I've been conducting a study since I arrived here."

"So that's where you head off to every morning. And, here, I thought you were attending some kind of law school program. You sure had me with the book bag and everything."

"No, I limit my ice cream sampling to afternoons, when class is over, and I have my tasting team with me."

"Have you and your team gotten to the finer points—flavor, type of cone, sprinkles or no sprinkles, kind of sprinkles?"

"Not yet, we're still working on hitting all the stands in the Tribeca area. On the serious side ..."

Nick tensed in anticipation of what Ava might be moving on to. He couldn't throw off the feeling that it would be something he didn't want to hear."

"This cone is filling, and I have a ton of homework tonight. So I'm going to beg off your supper invitation."

"Is that all?"

Ava frowned. "What were you expecting?"

"Nothing." The last thing he wanted was for her to know how insecure he was about her, them together. "I'm not sure I can take you standing me up on our second date."

"Second date?"

"Yeah, ice cream one and dinner, two."

"Oh, I think you'll have enough company for supper with four kids, Ellen and her daughter."

But not the company he wanted most. "All right."

They were approaching the restaurant. "But I'll walk you to your door first and backtrack to the restaurant."

"As any gentleman would." Ava tightened her arm on his waist. Or it felt to him like she did, so he was going with that.

Nick stopped at the front door of their apartment complex and glanced around. It was rush hour, but there wasn't much foot traffic on Murray Street. Besides, what were the chances anyone walking by would know either Ava or him?

Ava looked up at him. "Thank you for taking off this afternoon to go to the 9/11 memorial with me."

"It was my pleasure." He bent and kissed her goodbye for only a fraction of the time he would have liked to. There *were* in a public place.

"See you tomorrow after class."

He opened the door and Ava went in. He watched her until she reached the elevator and gave him a little wave before getting on. This afternoon had been pleasure—pure pleasure. And he realized, he hadn't the slightest pang about putting Ava before work, nor about putting his cellphone on do-not-disturb for everyone except Ellen for the afternoon.

Ellen and the kids weren't at the restaurant yet when he walked in. He told the hostess he was waiting for others and turned his phone on. Several missed calls popped up from a number he didn't recognize. He went to voice mail and saw three messages from the number. He tapped the first one.

Nick, this is Constance. I have a new phone number. We're home from our honeymoon. Call me. I need to talk with you about Mia and Lucas.

He dropped onto the bench by the hostess station. She wanted the twins back. They had become such a part of his life again that the thought of them going to Texas sucker punched him. Not only would their leaving tear his heart, but he also feared that Mia and Lucas might be what held him and Ava together. Their relationship was too new for him to be sure it wasn't.

Nick pressed Constance's number.

"Hello," she answered.

"It's Nick. About the twins. When do you want me to fly out with them?"

"You don't have to do that."

His heart lightened. Was she going to let them stay the rest of the summer? Or dare he hope longer?

Constance smashed his hopes to splinters. "The nanny I hired flew to New York this afternoon. She has the twins' tickets to Houston. The flight will let them get to know each other. All you need to do is meet her at JFK by 10:30 tomorrow morning."

"Tomorrow," he repeated.

"Yes. Let me give you her information."

Nick numbly punched it into his notes app on his phone before pulling himself together. "You're just back. I can keep them longer, let you get used to your new place. I'll reimburse you any charge for changing the flights and for your nanny's flight and fly back with them."

"No, we have to get a routine worked out before they start kindergarten and I go back to work. Anything they can't take on the plane, you can ship here in the crates they brought." Constance gave him her address. "I guess that's it. I've got to run." She hung up before he could say anymore.

Nick stared at his phone. He wanted to say he couldn't believe Constance would send someone Mia and Lucas didn't know to take them home. But he could. And there wasn't anything he could do about it. He had no rights to Mia and Lucas, no familial ties except his heart strings. He leaned his elbow to his knee, head to his palm. How was he going to tell the twins? How was he going to tell Ava?

He lifted his head and pressed Ava's number on his phone.

"I think you better join us for dinner," he said when she answered. "Constance is flying Mia and Lucas to Texas tomorrow."

12

———

*A*va woke up the next morning feeling as if she'd never gone to sleep. Nick had waited until they'd gotten back from eating with Ellen and her family before he'd told Mia and Lucas about them having to go home. To their new home with Constance and Carson. Ava rubbed her red eyes. They hadn't seemed to understand, or more likely bright as they were, they were stubbornly refusing to understand. While she and Nick got them ready for bed, they kept asking when they would be coming back.

After they were tucked in, with Ava having promised to be back early to help them pack, she and Nick had sat on the couch holding each other, just holding each other, hungry for any solace they could get.

She padded into the bathroom, showered, and washed her face with cold water before she attempted to put on a happy face, both makeup and attitude-wise. The pain she felt at Mia and Lucas leaving could only be a fraction of Nick's pain. She was determined to be there for all of them today.

Fifteen minutes later, she stepped into Nick's apartment. "How are they?" she asked nodding toward the bedroom where they must be."

"In denial, and I'm afraid I've made it worse. Trying to reassure them, I said I'd come visit them soon. Lucas studied the calendar on my desk and asked what day. You know how he is with numbers."

"Yes." It was one of many things that endeared the little boy to her. "We could make plans to go during the two weeks I have between my summer course and fall classes." It would be a stretch financially and might or might not be in everyone's best interest, but Mia and Lucas would have the reassurance that Nick wasn't abandoning them. "It's only a couple weeks away."

"You'd do that?" Nick asked.

"Yes, and not only for the twins."

Nick gave her a hug that Ava wished would never end.

When he did release her, she said with a sniffle she couldn't hide, "Let's go help the kids pack."

Mia and Lucas had clothes strewn all over the bed and floor as if they'd had a clothes fight, which very well might have been the case from the giggling Ava had heard coming from the bedroom when she'd been in Nick's arms. Pain pricked her. The twins definitely were not prepared for what was happening.

"Oh no!" she said as brightly as she could. "Was there a tornado in here?"

"Ms. Ava," Lucas said in all seriousness, "tornados can't happen inside a house without being outside." He pointed out the window to the sunny day.

Mia glared at them. "I don't know why we need to pack all our stuff to go visit Aunt Constance and Carson. He doesn't like us anyway."

Nick knelt in front of Mia. "You aren't just going to visit Aunt Constance. She wants you to come and live with her again."

"I don't want to," she sobbed. "Aunt Constance and Carson don't like us like you do."

The helpless look on Nick's face cracked Ava's heart as much as the little girl's tears.

Lucas rushed over and patted his sister's shoulder. "It's okay. Uncle Nick is going to come visit us."

"Yes." Nick's voice was rough. "Ms. Ava and I are making plans to come see how you're settling in at your new house."

"Told you," Lucas said.

Mia sniffled. "Can we come back with you if we don't like it?"

Nick looked to Ava. "Let's not get ahead of ourselves. You liked living with your aunt before, right?" Ava crossed her fingers that Mia would agree.

"Yes, at our old house when Carson wasn't there."

"But you miss her, don't you?" Nick asked.

"Yes. But couldn't we live with you and only visit Aunt Constance instead?"

"Or she could visit us here without Carson." Lucas offered. "We could show her all the places Ms. Ava took us."

In all of today's confusion, one thing was clear to Ava. There was something between the twins and Constance's husband.

Indecision flashed in Nick's eyes. Ava gave him a slight shake of her head *no*. He had to be honest with the twins. He couldn't make promises he couldn't keep.

"Don't you love us anymore?"

Mia's words were a low blow to her and Nick. Nick wrapped his arms around both the children and cleared his throat. "I love you more than anything. But sometimes we have to do things we don't want to. Can you understand?"

"Sort of," Lucas said.

"I can't just take you away from your aunt." Desperation clouded Nick's voice. "Aunt Constance and I will work something out."

"You won't stay away for a long time again?" Mia asked.

"No, and if it's okay with Aunt Constance, I can visit you on the computer if I can't come and visit in person. Would you like that?"

"Yes," both children said.

"Ms. Ava, too?"

"When I can." Lucas had put her on the spot. Her and Nick's relationship was too new to make any long-term promises.

"Ms. Ava is going to be busy with school. Just like you two are going to be busy with kindergarten."

She appreciated Nick giving her a hand, even though the reminder of fall classes brought her No

Brides vow to mind. Was she getting too involved, too fast with Nick and his life? She took a cleansing breath. That was a matter for another day. Today she needed to be here for the twins and him as much as she could.

Ava put on her brightest smile, even though she felt more like bursting into tears. "Okay, let's see who can get packed fastest, the boys or the girls."

Lucas tossed a wad of clothes from the floor in his suitcase.

"Neatly packed. Clothes folded," she said. "And wait until I say go."

"Okay." He took the wad out.

"Go!"

Once the suitcases were packed, boys winning because they were less neat at their folding, Ava and Nick took the cases and left them alone to pick out toys that would fit in their backpack carry-ons to take with them. Nick assured them he would send the rest.

Nick took her hands in his. "I can't thank you enough for coming this morning. You're sure it won't mess things up with your course?"

She squeezed his hand. "I needed to be here for me, as well as for you and the twins. I'm in good standing at school, as long as I make the afternoon session today and can finish the homework I didn't finish yesterday. I couldn't do anything after supper."

He pulled her to him and brushed her lips with his. "Did you get any sleep?"

"Not much," she admitted.

"Me either."

Nick's phone pinged with an update on their Uber ride. "Our ride is on the way," he called into the other room. "You guys ready?"

Lucas and Mia appeared in the doorway with their backpacks, looking closer to happy than they had when she and Nick and had left the bedroom. Uneasiness waved over her. She shook it off best she could. They *could* have resigned themselves. On the other hand, she couldn't put it past them to have plotted something for the airport.

Ava breathed a sigh of relief when they made it to the airport with no breakdowns. She and Nick found the nanny with no problems at the meeting place Constance had given him.

"Hello, I'm Nick Jansen. You must be Christina." He motioned to Ava. "And this is my friend Ava."

She gave Christina a once over. Dressed in business casual with her hair fastened neatly back in a French braid, the woman looked to be in her mid-thirties. Her nails were clipped short like Ava's, no polish.

"Hello," Christina said to both of them leaning forward toward the twins. "And you must be Mia and Lucas."

Suddenly shy, they mumbled, "Yes," and turned their faces into Nick's pant legs.

Seemingly understanding or at least satisfied with the kids' greeting, Christina said, "I'm sure you want to see my ID." She handed her license and a slip of paper to Nick.

He scrutinized the license and read the paper, which Ava assumed was a note from Constance. He nodded and handed the license back, a muscle working in his jaw. Then he squatted and picked up both children. "I need kisses and hugs to last me until I can get some more," he said.

They lavished him with affection.

"Ms. Ava, too," Lucas said.

Nick stepped close with the kids, and Ava kissed and hugged each of them, holding back the tears that pricked her eyes.

After another kiss and hug, Nick placed the twins back on the floor.

"We have to get in line for security," Christina

said, taking each child's hand, and giving them a gentle tug.

Mia and Lucas waved to her and Nick before taking a step. Halfway to the line, Mia jerked her hand away and ran back toward them. A second later, Lucas was behind her. Ava's stomach dropped. How was she going to be able to say goodbye again without losing it?

The little girl stopped short in front of them. "I forgot to say, love you Uncle Nick and Ms. Ava."

Lucas stopped beside her. "Love you, too, Uncle Nick and Ms. Ava."

"I—" Nick stopped and looked at her. "We love you."

Ava sniffled and nodded. Before she could collect herself or say anything, the twins turned and raced toward Christina and got in line without looking back.

"We'll stay until I can't see them anymore." Nick wrapped her in his arms.

Ava leaned into him with her assent. "Love you," she said, not knowing whether she'd said it to herself or out loud, or to the twins or to Nick.

She tightened her arms around his waist, feeling nothing but his strength. Nick kissed her on the head.

Out loud or to herself. It didn't matter which.

———

When the twins were obscured by the line behind them and Christina, Nick released Ava. "I don't know what I would have done without you here."

Ava squeezed his hand. "I couldn't let you come alone, or Mia and Lucas leave without my saying goodbye." Her voice cracked. "I don't know when I'll see them again."

"In a few weeks." Nick tried to console her as she'd consoled him by being there. Guilt nipped him. He didn't know that for sure. Constance could stop them.

Ava's smile didn't reach her eyes and her hand was limp in his. Something had shifted, and all he could think was Ava might put up a barrier between them.

"If it's all right with their aunt."

Nick was sure Ava was only grounding him, but her statement fed his doubts. "Do you have time for lunch before your need to be at the university?" he asked as they walked to the rental car.

"What time is it?"

Nick checked his phone. "It's about 11:00."

She bit her bottom lip and released it. "I have yesterday's assignment to finish before class this afternoon. I'd better go right home."

He flagged a taxi for them. "I understand." *But I don't want to be alone in the apartment this afternoon.* "How about dinner?"

Ava shook her head, her expression contrite. "It's Thursday. I have my No Brides meeting."

He should *not* feel jealous of a group of women he didn't know. Except these were all women who put their careers ahead of personal relationships. And it was a group encouraging Ava to do the same.

"Right," he answered belatedly. "I'm going to work at the club and probably work out after I finish." Anything to not have to face Mia and Lucas's toys in his bedroom yet.

"Sounds like a plan."

They rode in silence to the apartment complex. The taxi driver pulled into one of the five-minute parking spaces in front of their building.

"Thanks again for coming with me," Nick said.

Ava opened her door. "I went for me, too." She released a breath. "I didn't mean that like it came out. But I couldn't not have gone."

He squeezed her hand, resisting the impulse to

pull her into his arms and just hold her as he had last night.

She squeezed his hand back. *A good sign.* He debated whether to say he'd text her later or wait for her to say something. He didn't want to appear as needy as he felt.

Ava slipped out of the car. "Talk to you soon," she said before closing the door.

Nick watched her walk into the complex. When? He should have said something. He paid the driver and dragged himself into the athletic club office.

"Surprise!"

He jumped. "Aunt Sandy. What are you doing here?"

"Taking you to lunch. Your uncle and I flew in this morning. He has a lunch meeting with the attorney here who's working with our Buffalo attorney on the nonprofit incorporation."

He hung his head. "You called, and I had my phone on do-not-disturb." He clicked his phone on and saw her voicemail message.

"And texted. And left a message here at the club. The person on the front desk said you usually came in afternoons. So I decided to come and wait. We're only here for the day on our way to visit Adam and his family."

"I'm sorry."

"Not a problem. If you weren't here soon, I was going to have the club manager give me a tour to take up time while I waited."

Maggie. He'd barely seen her since he'd turned down her invitation for drinks, had talked by text when needed for work. He shook off guilt that he hadn't given her a thought with Ava around.

His aunt hitched her purse strap up on her shoulder. "So, where should we go? I saw a little restaurant just up the street when Pete dropped me off."

"No!" Nick said louder than he should have.

"That bad?" his aunt asked.

"No, it has great food." He might as well let it all out. Wasn't that what Ava had shown him? "Please sit."

His aunt took the chair in front of the empty desk they stood next to with a concerned expression, and he dropped into the chair behind it.

"We all had dinner there last night: me, Ava, the kids, and one of our neighbors and her grandchildren." Nick stopped to gather his thoughts.

Aunt Sandy placed her hand on his. "Something happened there."

He shook his head, and her expression became more confused.

"Mia and Lucas went back to their aunt Constance this morning. To Texas." His words came out in a torrent. "She sent a nanny, someone the twins had never met before to take them to Texas. Ava came with us to the airport. Afterwards she had to go to her classes."

Aunt Sandy's look of confused concerned turn to disapproval. "She left you alone? Just like that?"

"I told her to. I couldn't let her jeopardize her spot in law school because of me and my problems."

"I guess."

From her tone, his aunt clearly didn't understand Ava not being with him.

Aunt Sandy patted his hand. "Are you all right?"

"Not at all." I came into work hoping to occupy my mind with something else.

"The children?"

"They're in denial, thinking they'll have a choice to come back here." He couldn't keep the catch out of his voice. "In reality, I may never see them again."

"Couldn't you work out visitation? You could talk with Claire—"

"What good would it do? I'm no real relation to the twins. Constance is their biological aunt and guardian. She may even be in the process of adopting them. Or she and her new husband may be. She and I started the process when we were engaged, before she broke off the engagement and asked me not to contact the kids. I hadn't seen them in more than six months when she dropped them here at the club and took off on her honeymoon."

"She just dropped them off here with you?"

"Not directly with me. Constance left them in the club's Kids Korner childcare room with me as an alternate contact while she took a complimentary Tai Chi class. But she never returned from the class. That's how I met Ava. She was the substitute childcare worker that day." His thoughts traveled back to their meeting. He smiled. "And she wasn't very happy about having to track me down when her shift ended, and the room closed for dinner."

His aunt sputtered. "Just leaving them there like that has to be child endangerment or something. What if you hadn't taken them? You should talk with Claire."

"Constance's housekeeper, who was supposed to be caring for Mia and Lucas while Constance was honeymooning, quit. Constance knew I'd take care of them, although it would have been good to have some notice. She knows I love the twins."

"Then why did she cut off the kids' contact with you?"

"To spite me because I wouldn't change who I was for her." He shrugged. "I didn't say Constance wasn't self-centered."

"You're worried about them." It was a statement not a question.

"Some, and about what Ava and I told them this morning."

Aunt Sandy folded her hands on the desk. "What?"

Nick's chest tightened. "We said we'd come and visit them in Texas in a couple of weeks, after Ava's summer program finishes and that we'd chat with them on the computer.

"You know you'll have to come through on those?"

He glared at his aunt. Of course he did. What kind of man did Aunt Sandy think he was?

"I'm sorry. Your mother. Your upbringing."

Nick scoffed. "Mother didn't renege on what she said she'd do with me. She simply didn't offer much, and almost never things I wanted to do." His stomach rumbled. "Excuse me."

"You're hungry. We need to get lunch." Aunt Sandy stood and picked up her purse. "And what time does Ava get done with her class. I don't want to miss seeing her."

He stood and his aunt ushered him out of the office.

"We're staying until tomorrow morning and plan to see an off-Broadway play tonight that's been getting fantastic reviews. I thought you and Ava could come with us."

Nick struggled with determining whether his aunt was being presumptive, as his mother often was, assuming he and Ava would drop everything and go despite the short notice. Or if she was simply extending a family invitation to join them if he and Ava wanted to. "That sounds good to me." It beats working at the club all evening to avoid facing his empty apartment. "But I can't speak for Ava."

"I understand," Aunt Sandy said. "What time is her class over? You can give me her phone number, and I'll text her an invitation." She brushed her hands together. "Now back to the twins."

He pushed the club exit door open and held it for his aunt. "What about them?"

"Your talking with Claire about what your options are for keeping in touch with them, you and Ava visiting Mia and Lucas later this summer."

"I think my only option is to try and stay on good terms with Constance."

"That couldn't hurt, but you may be able to have more."

The toe of Nick's shoe caught on the uneven edge of a crack in the sidewalk, causing him to stop abruptly to avoid tripping. Since the weekend in Western New York, every time he thought of Mia and Lucas, Ava was also in the picture. They'd become a package deal in his mind. But Ava had other plans for this evening. He couldn't accept a theater ticket from his aunt on Ava's behalf.

Nick started walking again. He was going to have to do something about his uncertainty.

———

Ava walked home from the Briarwood Tavern to clear her head and think about the No Brides Club meeting. All the members at the meeting sympathized with her about the twin's sudden departure. Vivian and a couple others said it was unfortunate she'd lost work she enjoyed that fit in her summer schedule so well. Vivian had also thought caring for Mia and Lucas balanced Ava's law studies.

Some of the longer-term members expressed opinions that the twins leaving was for the best. As long as she wasn't dependent on the income, not working would let her devote all of her time to her studies.

"Hey lady. Watch where you're going," a taxi driver honked and shouted out the car window when Ava stepped off the curb against the light. She leapt back, heart pounding, as it had when she'd spoken at the meeting. Because of the responses she'd gotten and her sister not being there, Ava hadn't said anything about her growing attraction to Nick. Nor had she asked for advice about handling it, as she'd planned to.

And now she was angry at herself for not asking, for thinking she needed Kate there for support, for not being able to act on her own. She strode ahead of the crowd when the traffic light changed weighing the No Brides Club creed against Nick's cousin Claire having achieved what Ava wanted with a husband and a baby. Maybe that was the key, Claire had had the all-consuming start-up phase of being a couple out of the way when she was in law school. *Well*, she didn't, and she had enough to do proving to her family and herself she could tackle law school without adding a romantic relationship with Nick.

As much as she would like to under different circumstances.

Ava reached to pull open the door to the apartment complex and grabbed air before stumbling into a warm, sturdy, male form. The man wrapped his arms around her, and Ava's thoughts jumped between whether she could get her spray mace out of her purse or knee him.

Then the man chuckled. "A thank you for opening the door would have been sufficient, but I like this better. Much better." Nick's breath tickled her ear and sent a spark through her that burned out any thought of keeping Nick at a distance, along with any other thoughts she had.

A "get a room" look from a guy who wanted to enter the building snapped Ava and Nick out of their cocoon. They moved out of the doorway.

Ava took a deep breath to ground herself. "I thought you were going to a play with your aunt and uncle this evening. Had he passed it up because she'd had to decline his aunt's invitation because of her meeting? Her heart warmed until her better sense told her she was losing it.

"I was. But there was a bomb threat and the block where the theater is had to be evacuated. Tonight's show was cancelled. The news alert said tonight's tickets could be used for another performance or be refunded." Nick walked her to the elevator, and she pressed the button.

"Are your aunt and uncle going to see the play tomorrow, then?" she asked while they waited.

"No, they're expected at my cousin Adam's. They can only stay tonight."

Nick and Ava stepped into the elevator, just the two of them. Ava took a small step back away from Nick and the unusual feeling of confinement she'd gotten when the elevator doors had closed "That's too bad. Someone in class was talking about the play during break. It sounded like it's gotten good reviews."

"Did the play sound like something you'd like to see?"

"Seeing a New York play *is* on my list of things to do while I'm here."

The elevator stopped at their floor, and Nick waited for her to exit fist.

"Well, you can cross that off your list," he said stepping into the hall.

"Pardon?"

"You can cross off seeing a New York play from your list. Aunt Sandy gave me their tickets."

"Oh! Is that an invitation?" she teased.

"Yes. Date three."

"I'd love to see it," Ava said before she could think that seeing the play together would only encourage their relationship—on both sides.

Nick walked her to her apartment door. "Tonight and tomorrow night are sold out. I checked. But there's 7:30 show on Sunday."

Ava fiddled with unlocking her door while Nick waited for an answer. Her thoughts went to her No Brides meeting.

"Do you have something else going on?" Nick struck a casual pose, leaning against the wall next to the door, that looked anything but casual.

She couldn't lie to him. She had nothing planned for the weekend except household chores and studying. "No. Sorry. My key didn't seem to be working"—*because I tried to insert it upside down.* "I'd love to go. If you want, I can make us supper here before." What was she doing? Her invitation was taking her further from her No Brides vow. Ava turned the doorknob before looking over and up at Nick. His wide grin hit her like a missile. "Nothing fancy," she warned as soon she'd righted herself from the attack.

"Anything is fine if it means spending time with

you." He pushed himself off the wall. "What time for dinner?"

"It sounds early, but, say 5:30." She pushed her door open. "One more thing."

"What?" he waited.

"If this is a date, you might want to brush up on your pick-up lines."

"I didn't wow you with that one?"

Ava just laughed and waved bye over her shoulder as she crossed the threshold into her apartment. She stopped on the other side of the closed door. But he had gotten to her with his corny line.

More than she'd ever admit to him—or to herself.

13

———

$\mathcal{N}$ick would never have thought he'd be grateful for a bookkeeping error but having to go to Pennsylvania overnight to straighten it out with one of the clubs had helped him get through the first two whole days sans the twins without thinking about them too much.

Nick unlocked the door and let himself into his apartment, an apartment that had become way too quiet. He missed the chaos only Lucas and Mia could create. Tossing his overnight bag and briefcase on the couch, he glanced at the clock on the DVR. He had just enough time to send his revised report to his uncle and get ready for his date with Ava. And in contrast to their first two "dates," this was a real one. He whipped off his report to his uncle and hit the shower.

He stepped out, toweled his hair dry, and rubbed his chin. He'd forgotten his razor, so he hadn't shaved this morning at the hotel. Should he go with the stubble look? Women were supposed to go for that, weren't they? He glanced in the mirror. *Nah,* he'd better shave. Clean shaven was how Ava was used to seeing him.

Now, suit or something more casual? The theater was a stately old building off Broadway that his mother would say called for evening wear. Maybe he should check with Ava to see what she was wearing. He dragged his fingers though his freshly combed hair. What was with him? It wasn't as if this was the first time he'd taken a woman to a play. Nick threw open his closet door and stilled. But it was the first time he'd be taking Ava, and he wanted to look good. For her.

More than that, he wanted her to be comfortable with him. With date Nick. Not Uncle Nick. Not businessman Nick. He pulled out a sports jacket, dress pants, and a pale blue oxford shirt. No tie. *There was nothing wrong with wanting to look nice,* he assured himself.

When he returned to the living room and checked the time, it was only 5:15. He shook his hands and rolled his shoulders. Ava wasn't expecting him until 5:30. He could work off some of his nervous energy by walking the stairs to the lobby and back up. But that might get him all sweaty. He picked up his phone from the coffee table in front of the couch, thinking to call Constance to talk with Mia and Lucas and shoved it into his pocket. Tonight was his and Ava's time. Besides, Constance had texted him when the kids had arrived asking him to give them a few days to settle in before calling. But she hadn't seemed to have any objections to him calling in general. After pacing the room a few times, Nick gave up. Ava would just have to put up with him being early.

"Hi," Ava said swinging the door open. Her smiling countenance bedazzled his vocal cords unusable and sent his pulse into double-time. Highlighted by a splash of turquoise on the lids, her always expressive eyes were more attention-drawing than usual. Turquoise earring dangled from her lobes almost to her shoulders. Crimson lipstick made her lips nearly too tempting to resist, but he restrained himself. He hadn't even said hello.

"Come on in. You're a little early."

He shrugged. "I was ready." What was he, fourteen?

"I was about to take the meatloaf and baked potatoes out of the oven."

He dropped his gaze to avoid hers and regroup his composure and broke into laughter instead. Ava had on an oversized Buffalo Bills jersey that reached almost to her knees with a couple inches of shiny cloth making a fringe below it.

"Like it?" she asked with a lopsided smile.

"Personally, I think the Eagles green would go better with the turquoise than the blue."

She playfully slapped his arm. Nick relaxed. This was more like it. He hadn't been sure he could have lasted the whole evening as keyed up as he'd been.

"I wanted to be all dressed for supper, but didn't have an apron to protect my dress, so I improvised with my night shirt." Ava turned to go into the kitchen area behind the counter separating it from the living room.

Nick ran his gaze down her back, taking in how the jersey skimmed her curves. He swallowed. Hard. "I'll take the food out of the oven if you want to ... uh ... finish dressing."

"Since you've already seen my lovely cooking ensemble, do you mind if I keep the jersey on while we eat so I don't drip catsup or something on my dress."

Nick took in Ava's bare arms under the jersey's sleeves. "That's fine." *More than fine. Yeah.* Hold off on the full impact of the dress Nick was imaging under the jersey until he had some food in him and more time to get himself on an even keel.

They had a whole evening ahead, just the two of them.

———

"Sit. I can manage." Her apartment had the same setup as Nick's with an eating nook in one corner of the living room. Not only could she manage, but it would put some distance between them. She'd done fine holding down her nervousness until she'd slapped Nick's forearm. It was a good thing he had on his jacket. With the hum touching his jacket sleeve had set off, she wasn't sure she could have handled touching his warm skin.

When she carried over the platter of meat and potatoes, Nick had taken off his jacket and laid it over the back of the chair to his right. "You look nice." She blurted the first thing that came into her head.

"Do you think I need a tie? I have one in my jacket pocket."

Ava's gaze dropped to the V of his open shirt collar and to a fine brown curl peeping over the V. "No, you look great." She all but dropped the platter in front of him. "I'll just get the green beans." Ava whirled around and took refuge behind the counter, which she wanted to grasp while she took several deep breaths but couldn't with Nick watching her. She had her pride, couldn't let him see how he unsettled her.

"Here you go. Dig in." Ava placed the beans on the table and slid into the chair across from Nick.

He speared a slice of the meatloaf. "Are you feeling weird?"

Ava picked up her fork. *So much for trying to hide it.*

"I am," he said before she could answer. "We've eaten supper together enough times, albeit with the twins. Let's pretend it's a regular evening."

A weight lifted from her shoulders "I'm for that. So, how was your day?"

They talked through the meal until, almost too soon, it was time to leave for the theater. Nick helped her clear the table and carry the dishes to the kitchen sink.

"I'll ditch the jersey, grab my wrap, and we can leave." Ava went to her bedroom and returned with a silver threaded pashmina and matching evening bag on her arm. "All set."

Wide-eyed, Nick whistled. "Suspending the average evening thing. You look beautiful." He ran his gaze up her body to her face. "That around the neck ..." He motioned to the dress' halter and her shoulders. "That's why I didn't see any sleeves. You know, sticking out below the jersey sleeves."

Ava burst out laughing. "Thank you, and I think we're back to a regular evening."

Nick reached for his sports jacket and stopped. "It's a warm evening. Do you mind if I leave my jacket here and pick it up when we get back?"

"I don't mind, if you're more comfortable without it."

Nick's phone pinged. He reached down and pulled it from his jacket pocket. "That's our ride. Let's go."

They walked hand-in-hand out to the car. A few minutes later, as they walked into the theater, Ava said, "Can I make a confession?"

A startled look preceded Nick's hesitant reply, "Sure."

"I was in every play my high school drama club

presented, but I've never been to a professional performance."

"Is that all?" Nick said.

"Yes. What did you expect?"

He shrugged.

"And lest you think we Lewises are totally uncultured hicks—"

"I don't," he interrupted. "I'd never ..."

"Tickets, please."

Nick handed their tickets to the usher.

Ava patted his arm. "I'm teasing. Mom and Dad always went to at least one Artpark play in Buffalo every summer." She felt herself blushing. "I guess I kind of thought plays were something older people went to. But I'm so excited about seeing this play ... with you."

"Welcome to the older crowd," Nick said stopping at their row and chuckling before motioning her in."

Before she stepped into the row, Ava looped her arm around his and hugged her head to his shoulder. "Thank you for recognizing that."

A flash of confusion passed across Nick's face when she let go and looked up. Ava let it pass. Now wasn't the time to get into her baggage. It was the time to enjoy herself, the play, and the company. She sat and rested her left arm palm up on the arm rest between her and Nick's seats.

He sat and curled his fingers between hers.

A warm calm encased her. She was already enjoying herself and the company. She squeezed Nick's hand and he squeezed hers back. Definitely enjoying the company.

As she and Nick clapped with the rest of the audience for a third standing ovation, Ava murmured "Amazing," for the third time.

"So you liked it," Nick said dryly.

"I loved it, and you know it. So stop gloating." Ava turned and lifted her wrap from the armrest.

Nick stepped into the aisle and let her out, placing his hand on the small of her back while they walked to the exit.

An array of stars Ava could see despite the city lights welcomed them into the warm night where their Uber was waiting.

Nick opened the back door to let her in first. "Would you like to stop for a drink somewhere near the apartment building and walk home? Enjoy the beautiful night."

And extend her evening with him. Ava thought of the Briarwood Tavern. It was a nice walk from there to home. But that was another part of her life that she should keep separate from her and Nick. At least for a while. "I'd like to walk part of the way, but I'm going to pass on the drink. I have to get up early, remember." *And I hardly slept last night thinking about tonight.*

"Okay."

Ava thought she heard disappointment in his voice, and her heart swelled.

"I'll ask the driver to let us off in front of the Briarwood," Nick said, making her wonder if he'd read her thoughts. She hoped not, since he'd also have read the rest.

He put his arm around her shoulders, and she rested her head against him. What did she care if he knew she liked him, how much she enjoyed being with him? It was the truth.

The driver let them out in front of the Briarwood, and before she knew it Nick was walking her to her door.

He waited while she unlocked the door. "Have I told you what a good time I had this evening?" he asked.

She turned the doorknob and looked up at him. "Only about the same number of times I've told you what a wonderful time I had." Nick leaned toward her as if to kiss her goodnight. She wasn't ready for the evening to be over. "Your jacket," she said.

He jerked back.

Ava pushed the door all the way open. "You need to come in and get your jacket."

"Oh, yeah." He followed her in, grabbing her hand, he pulled her toward him and shut the door with his foot in one smooth motion. "I've been waiting, wanting to do this all evening," he whispered as his lips sampled, then devoured hers.

Ava closed her eyes and threw her arms around his shoulders, kissing him back with the same fervor before she lost herself in his taste, his feel.

Nick gentled the kiss while urging her closer with a gentle caress of her back.

His cell phone rang, bursting Ava's bubble of emotion.

"Ignore that." Nick renewed his kiss, but Ava couldn't regain the magic. He finished with a peck on the tip of her nose that almost reignited the flame that had drawn her to him. But she was too distracted.

"It was only my uncle. I thought I had everyone on do-not-disturb." Nick continued to hold her in his arms a while longer. "I guess I should get going. See you tomorrow."

He held her at arms-length now, his hands resting on her shoulders as if he wasn't ready to let go completely. She swallowed at the realization that she wasn't, not by a long shot. "Not until late afternoon," she got out in a raspy voice that seemed to send a shiver through him. She cleared her throat. "I'm going shopping with Ellen after class to help her pick out clothes for the cruise she's taking."

Nick squeezed her shoulders, dropped his hands, and lightly brushed her lips. "I'd better go while I'm still able."

His rough voice turned her boneless. Before she could act, he'd opened the door and stepped into the hall.

"Goodnight," Ava whispered as she closed the door behind him, making her way to the kitchen table for support. No one had ever kissed her like that before. She grabbed his sports jacket from the chair back and pulled it on as if to recapture a part of the feeling of being in his arms.

What was she going to do? She was falling in love with Nick. Ava rubbed the lapel of the jacket between her fingers. No, make that past tense.

She *had* fallen in love with him.

14

Ava's smile. Her expressive eyes. Her softness under his hands. The sweet yield of her lips on his.

"And now Nick will run through the financial details with you," Uncle Pete said.

Nick jumped as if this were the real meeting and not a run-through they were doing of the presentation they were giving tomorrow in Chicago. "I ... I ... They aren't complete," he admitted before looking at his laptop screen and seeing that they were. Uncle Pete must have finished them when he took a break to call Ava last night. She certainly had him not knowing which way was up.

"Sorry," Nick said.

"Don't be. I remember when your aunt and I

were young. How I felt every minute I was away from her. Three days could feel like three weeks. Still feel that way." His uncle laughed.

"How did you know? You know, that you were in love with Aunt Sandy?"

"What I just said, plus an inkling that she felt the same. And the sensation that my whole world had been turned upside down—in a good way."

"I'm a goner," Nick said.

"Then, we'd better get this presentation together for tomorrow, so you can get back to New York and Ava."

Nick hesitated, not remembering the last time he'd been so uncertain. "What if Ava doesn't feel the same?"

"I saw you two at the party. I don't think that's going to be a problem."

Nick's heart soared. Then plummeted. *That's when Mia and Lucas were still with him.*

A couple of run-throughs later, Nick and his uncle had the presentation perfect.

"Let's go see what we can rummage up for lunch," his uncle said.

A notification that he had a video call popped up on Nick's laptop. "I've got a call. You go ahead."

"Ah, the lovely Ava."

No, it was from Constance's area code. But he went along with his uncle's tease and clicked the notification.

"Hi, Uncle Nick." First Mia's and, then, Lucas's face appeared on his screen.

"How? I mean, hi, guys."

"Aunt Constance got us a tablet," Lucas said.

Lucas, at least, had gone back to calling Constance aunt. The first few days they'd been with him, they'd both referred to her as Mommy the times they mentioned her at all. His stomach clenched.

Mia huffed. "We have to share the tablet."

"I watched Aunt Constance when she set up the tablet stuff," Lucas said. "And I know your phone number."

Nick wasn't going to ask how.

"You didn't call us. So we called you," Mia finished for her brother.

"It's good to see you two. I miss you. What have you been doing?" Nick thought that was a better question than the others ricocheting around his head: *Are you happy? Are you getting along with Carson? Who's watching you that you were able to make this call without them knowing?* Constance had asked him to hold off on video calling for a couple of weeks so the twins could adjust to being back with her—and to not book flights for him and Ava to visit yet.

"We haven't been doing nothing," Lucas said.

"Yeah, not like with Ms. Ava," Mia said.

"Ms. Christina doesn't take us anywhere, like Ms. Ava did," Lucas uncharacteristically complained. "And Mia hasn't even done anything very bad."

"That's good to hear." *I think.*

"Is Ms. Ava there with you?" Mia asked.

Both twins looked around behind Nick before Mia said, "You're not at your house."

"No I'm working with my uncle Pete at his house for a few days."

"Who's staying with Ms. Ava?" Lucas asked.

No one, Nick hoped. "She's at class right now, with her friends."

That seemed to satisfy them.

"What are you two doing?" Constance appeared behind the kids.

"Talking with Uncle Nick," Lucas said.

Constance glared at him.

"Hey, don't blame me. They made the call." Nick couldn't help meeting her glare with a smile.

"How?"

"Lucas figured it out."

Constance's glare was replaced by exasperation. "You two go downstairs. Ms. Christina has a snack ready for you. I need to talk to Uncle Nick. Say goodbye to him,"

"Bye," the twins said, their reluctance to go clear in their expressions.

"Sorry," Nick said. "When I saw the area code, I felt I should pick up."

Constance shook her head. "I was going to call you anyway. Do you and your friend, the highly lauded, Ms. Ava still plan to come visit."

He rolled his eyes. "Yes."

"Good. Sooner might be better than later. Christina isn't clicking with the twins. Lucas and Mia are all Ms. Ava this and Ms. Ava that. I thought while you were visiting, she could help me interview for a new nanny."

"I guess," Nick said. "Ava has a week and a half of classes left. I could look into flights for the week after if you want."

"Perfect." Constance audibly released a breath. "Christina has given her two-weeks' notice."

"Oh." He hesitated. "How are you?"

"In general, great. Really. I'm happy. Carson makes me happy. I make him happy. This is the real thing, although he's still adjusting to the little terrors."

"I'm glad, you've found what you want." Nick tried to not read too much into Constance's last comment. Anyone would need a little time to adjust to the twins,

"And you?" Constance asked.

"Aside from missing the kids, I'm good. I have the work for my uncle almost wrapped up, and I've reconnected with him and his family."

"You always wanted family. So that is good," Constance said. "Let me know about your visit when you have the dates worked out."

"I will. Ava will probably want to video call with the kids since she missed out on today's call." Not that he'd had much of a conversation with them, either.

"Fine. Just give me a heads-up on a time."

"I can do that." A scream came loud and clear through the phone.

"I've got to go." A blank square replaced Constance's face.

Nick stood to go join his uncle for lunch. A strong urge to talk with Ava stopped his movement. He pulled his phone out of his pocket. She'd still be in class. He punched in a quick text.

Miss you!

Nick shook his head. He had it bad. The next thing he knew he'd be adding colorful emojis to his texts. Shoving his phone back in his pocked, Nick headed toward the kitchen. He had a lot to say to Ava when he called her this evening. His thoughts went back to the conversation he'd had with Uncle Pete, and his heart hammered against his chest wall in anticipation and trepidation.

An awful lot.

———

*A*va peeked through the peephole in her apartment door and swung the door open. "Nick. What are you doing here?"

He laughed, and her hand went to her hair before smoothing the old t-shirt she had on over her sweatpants. She must look a mess.

"Is that any way to greet me after I've been gone for days."

"Three days, to be exact. Come in. I thought your flight was tomorrow. That's what you said last night." Ava shivered. Along with an *I love you* before he hung up. Hung up before she could say anything in return.

Nick's gaze went to the books and papers she had strewn over the couch and coffee table. "I didn't mean to interrupt your studying, but I couldn't wait to see you."

He opened his arms, and she stepped into them. Nick wrapped his arms around her in a warm hug that blocked out everything except Nick. She reluctantly stepped back when he released her.

"Am I disturbing you?" he asked.

That was an understatement.

"I mean your studying," he added as if picking up on her thoughts.

"Yes," she blurted. "I mean. I'm a little behind on my work. Ellen didn't find what she wanted when we went shopping on Monday, and she called me this morning to go with her again. I have part of yesterday's assignment and today's to finish."

"I can go, or I could stay and quietly watch the ballgame. I just want to be with you."

Ava stepped forward and pressed her lips lightly to his, unprepared for the heat that shot through her. "Stay. I want to be with you, too." She motioned to the recliner and scurried to unbury the TV remote from under a paper while she found her voice again. "Here you go."

Nick purposely brushed her fingers with his

while he took the remote. Or so it seemed to her. She had had their reunion tomorrow all planned out. And that plan hadn't had a tenth of the intensity his showing up tonight had.

Once Nick had settled in the recliner and turned on the TV, turning the volume very low, Ava started to get more of a grip on herself. She picked up the book she'd been reading. Should she offer him something to eat or drink? She started to place the book open side down on the table and rise. *No.* She had to put herself, her studies first. "If you're thirsty or hungry, the refrigerator is open game," she gave in partly.

"Thanks, I'm good for now."

Ava studied his profile before resettling her book on her lap. So was she good with him beside her? *Very good.*

A while later, she jotted notes on her legal pad and, sensing Nick's gaze on her for the umpteenth time, stuck her pen over her ear and gazed back. "What do you keep looking at?" she asked. Did she have sauce on her face from the cold pizza she'd had for supper?

"You," Nick said softly. "You're beautiful."

"I'm a mess," she countered, fluffing her hair as if that would help and causing her pen to go flying.

His gaze softened, if that were possible. "Your beauty is so much more than looks."

Ava fumbled for her pen on the floor as an excuse to break their eye contact.

"The way you are with Lucas and Mia, with my family." He laughed. "The way you put up with me, like letting me stay this evening. Your dedication to your studies. The way you balance that with life. You're going to make a terrific lawyer."

Ava's head shot up. "You think I'm going to make a terrific lawyer?"

"You absolutely are."

Nick believed in her and her ambition. Ava's heart soared. He was the only one who she was sure believed in her and her ability to complete law school. She rose wordlessly, walked to the recliner, sat on the arm, and leaned over to kiss him. "Thanks," she said against his warm lips. "I love you." *There.* She got it out as much for her as for Nick.

She let out a startled. "Yip!"

He pulled her to his lap. "I love you, too." He picked up the kiss where she'd left off.

When he ended the kiss, Ava snuggled against his hard chest, feeling both protected and energized by the security being in his arms gave her.

Nick kissed the top of her head, and Ava stayed where she was. She was close enough to done with her coursework for the night.

She didn't know how long they sat like that, only that it wasn't long enough when a cheer rose from the crowd, interrupting her peace.

Nick sat up straight, his chin bumping her head. "Yes! Walk off grand slam for the Phillies." He gazed down at her. "We won!"

Ava squeezed the arm he still had tightly around her, "We definitely have," she murmured.

15

ould life be better? Nick thought as he paced the living room waiting for Ava to arrive Sunday afternoon for their first video call together with the twins. He and Ava had fallen into a comfortable coupleness he'd never experienced before, the sale of Uncle Pete's clubs and the nonprofit set-up were almost completed, and out of the blue his mother had given him a real business lead in Boston. He hadn't fully interpreted her underlying motive yet.

The call rang early on his laptop. He strode over and answered. Constance appeared on the screen. "I couldn't get them to wait any longer," she said as Ava's knock sounded on the door.

"Hang on. That's Ava." He motioned to the door.

"I'll put the kids on while you answer the door," Constance said.

Nick opened the door and Ava stepped in. "Hi," he said closing the door behind her and leaning in for a quick kiss before thinking, *the kids are watching.* He took in Ava's soft expression and smile. *So what?*

"The twins are already on. Constance said they couldn't wait."

"Me either. I was ready fifteen minutes ago, and then Mom called. I finally got off by promising to ask if she and Dad can talk with the twins sometime."

Nick put his arm around Ava's shoulders, and they walked to the couch.

"Ms. Ava! Uncle Nick!" Mia and Lucas launched into a torrent of chatter that warmed his heart almost as much as listening to Ava's replies. He barely got a word in himself.

A half-hour later, Constance reappeared. "Okay, guys, time to say goodbye."

Nick opened his mouth to say he didn't mind talking longer. He snapped it shut. Constance was the custodial parent, and he didn't want to get on her bad side. "Bye, guys. Love you," he said instead.

"Bye Uncle Nick and Ms. Ava," Mia said.

"I love you, Uncle Nick and Ms. Ava," Lucas followed suit.

Ava blinked her eyes and cleared her throat. "Bye. I wish I could give each of you a big hug and kiss."

"Like Uncle Nick gave you?" Mia asked.

Ava's faint blush charmed him. "Yes, like that. Bye, guys." He ended the call, and his phone rang almost immediately after.

He looked at his phone. "Constance," he said without thinking.

"Want me to leave?" Ava offered.

"You don't have to. It's probably about our visit plans." His throat tightened. *Or any number of other things.* "Hi," he answered.

"Sorry," Constance said. "Hope I'm not interrupting anything."

"No, Ava and I are just going to watch the Phillies game."

"About your visit," Constance started.

"We don't have firm dates yet."

"Don't ... don't buy tickets."

Nick's heart in his throat almost choked him. "Why not?" he demanded.

Ava pointed at herself and, then, the door.

He shook his head as he got hold of himself.

"It looks like Carson's company is going to transfer him to London for a year."

A year was a long time to not see Mia and Lucas. "We could come as soon as next weekend to visit," he said, looking at Ava.

She nodded.

"No. Carson has to go tomorrow, and I'm going with him to find a house to rent."

Nick's temper ignited. "Tomorrow?"

"Calm down. I'm bringing Mia and Lucas to you. We're flying to London out of JFK."

"Oh. When do they have to be back?"

"Don't hate me," Constance said.

"Why would I hate you?"

"They don't have to be back. It's not working out. For Carson. Or me. I took them mostly because I thought I should." There was a thick pause. "I love them. I do. But not like you love and enjoy them. They love you and Ava." Constance was babbling and crying now. "Don't hate me," she repeated. "I can only be the twins' aunt."

"I don't hate you." He tried to calm her enough to figure out what she was saying, what she wanted of him.

Constance took a ragged breath and slowed her words enough to be coherent.

Nick heard her out. "I understand. Carson gives you what I couldn't. I'm glad for you...Yes, I will. Talk with you tomorrow." He hung up and stared at his phone a while before he looked over at Ava.

"A problem?" she asked.

He grinned before panicking that he didn't know how Ava would feel about that now that their relationship had deepened.

"Not for me. Constance is giving me custody of Mia and Lucas. Permanently, if I want it."

Ava threw her arms around him. "That's wonderful."

His panic fled at her touch.

"When?" she asked.

"Tomorrow. She's bringing the legal papers with her. She and Carson are flying out of JFK to London to check out housing. He's being transferred there."

Her arms loosened. "I can't watch them this week. My final."

Nick took her hands. "I know. I wouldn't ask you to. I'll make arrangements with the Kids Korner at the club or stay with them myself. You'll have your week to study."

"You understand. You get me."

Nick heard the importance in her words.

Her gaze held his. "I love you."

"I love you, too. With all my heart," he said before he remembered he hadn't told her about his trip to Boston. He'd planned to leave Thursday night.

But he could leave early Friday morning. *Yeah, it would all work out.*

He pulled Ava back into his arms, his heart overflowing.

It was sappy, but couldn't love conquer all?

———

*A*va had hardly seen Nick or the twins all week. True to his word—maybe a little too true—Nick had left her to her studying for her final. She'd had supper with them Monday evening after the twins' arrival, and that had been it, except for a short daily phone call, in which he assured her each day that the twins could wait until this evening to see her. Ava didn't know about them, but she was more than ready to have the twins over tonight. If she wasn't ready for her final tomorrow by now, she never would be.

Giggling and loud voices outside preceded the knock on the door. Ava swung it open and the kids rushed in on either side of her and hugged her legs.

"I missed you sooo much," Lucas said.

"I missed you more," Mia said.

"It's only been a couple of days, but I've missed you, too." *And your uncle even more.*

"Hi." Nick leaned forward and brushed her lips with his.

"Ick. You're not going to do that all the time like Aunt Constance and Carson, are you?" Lucas asked.

"Of course they are," Mia said. "They're in looove."

"Do I still have time to change my mind?" Ava leaned her head toward the twins.

Nick's face lost its *tan*. "You *are* teasing, I hope."

She patted his hand as an excuse to touch him again. "I'm teasing."

Nick wiped his forehead in an exaggerated whew! "They have their pajamas and clothes for tomorrow in their backpacks. "Thanks again for helping me."

"You're welcome. You know I want to."

"Okay." He scuffed the toe of his shoe on the carpet. "Promise me you'll drop the twins at the Kids Korner early enough in the morning to have time for yourself, to get ready for your exam."

"I promise. I made plans to meet some of the others for coffee and last-minute studying before our test."

"Good. I told Maggie at the club that I should be

able to pick Lucas and Mia up by about three tomorrow afternoon. I'll see you when you get home from your exam." Nick's eyes darkened as they did when he was about to kiss her. He jerked straight. "Mia and Lucas, go put your backpacks in the bedroom,"

"Yuck, Uncle Nick is going to kiss Ms. Ava again."

"Do as your uncle said, the same room as you stayed in last time. And no he's not going to kiss me."

"All right."

Ava waited until the kids disappeared into the other room. Then, she placed her hands on Nick's shoulders and lifted herself on her toes. Pinning his gaze with hers, she whispered, "I'm going to kiss Uncle Nick."

He chuckled, which Ava promptly silenced with her lips.

She broke the kiss when she heard little footsteps.

"I'd better go now, while I still can," he said, his voice raspy.

"Yes, you'd better, or I might have to kidnap you and not let you go to Boston."

"Hold that thought for another time." Nick ducked out the door to her laughter.

The next morning, the click of her bedroom door opening woke Ava. She blinked at the sun streaming through the split in the curtains.

"Ms. Ava. Ms. Ava. Are you awake?"

Ava pulled herself up to a sitting position in the bed. "I am now."

Lucas stared at her with a worried look on his face. "The big hand is on the twelve and the little hand is on the nine. You said we were getting up when the little hand was on the eight."

Ava sprung out of bed. Her coffee group was meeting at 10:00. "Is Mia awake?"

Lucas nodded.

"Good. The two of you get dressed and meet me at the kitchen table." Ava couldn't believe she'd slept so late. She'd had trouble falling asleep at first last night but had been dead to the world by midnight. She threw on jeans and a t-shirt and texted one of her study group friends she'd be late, figuring on coming back to the apartment to shower and get ready for the day after she dropped the twins at the Kids Korner.

"What do you say to a granola bar and juice for

breakfast?" she asked when she got to the kitchen area.

"Do they have raisins? I don't like raisins," Mia whined.

Ava bit her tongue not to snap at the little girl. She hated being rushed or late. "I think I have one with no raisins."

She pulled a variety pack of granola bars out of the cupboard and pulled out a bar that didn't have raisins for Mia. She let Lucas pick from the others while she got them each a juice box and their lunches from the refrigerator. Lunches they'd packed last night so they wouldn't be rushed this morning.

The twins dawdled with their breakfast to the extent it got Ava tapping her foot. They'd made it clear to her last night that they weren't happy about going to the Kids Korner again today. "Come on. You can eat your bars on the way to the club and bring your juice boxes with you, too."

"Do we have to?" Mia said.

"Yes you have to." Ava shook her hands and rolled her shoulders to shake off some of her tension. She needed to be relaxed for her exam.

A half hour later, she had the kids dropped off with no problems, had showered, dressed, put her makeup on, and was opening the door to the coffee shop where they were meeting. She greeted her friends, ordered her morning coffee—she'd switch to herbal tea later—and a muffin. Her phone pinged.

Good Luck! I'm heading to my meeting, Nick texted.

Thanks, good luck with your meeting, she typed in, stopped and, then, added. Love you.

Love you, too.

Ava smiled and joined in the study conversation. Two hours later, after a light lunch, she packed her things to head to the exam. As she stood and hoisted her bag to her shoulder, her phone buzzed, and she frowned. She'd thought she'd put everyone's number, except the Kids Korner, on do-not-disturb. She pulled her phone from her bag. It *was* the Kids Korner. She tensed. Whatever the twins—Mia—had done, they'd have to handle it. Ava started to drop the phone back into her bag but couldn't. Her heart leapt to her throat. What if it was an emergency?

"Hello," she answered.

"Ava, Ava Lewis?"

"Yes, I'm Ava."

"This is Maggie O'Shay from the Jansen Athletic club."

Some of Ava's tension seeped out. It was Maggie,

not someone from the Kids Korner. "What has Mia done now?" She didn't need this right now. "Whatever it is, you're going to have to handle it until their uncle gets there this afternoon. Or you could call him."

"Mia did a backflip off the picnic table, landed wrong and broke her leg, possibly in two places," Maggie answered. "The EMTs are here. You can meet them at Children's Hospital if you want. Maggie's voice turned smug. "And I did call Nick, His phone is on do-not-disturb." She hung up.

Ava stared at her phone. Poor little Mia. Fleetingly, she thought about calling Ellen to go to the hospital to be with Mia until she or Nick could get there. She still had twenty minutes to get to her final. Ava shook her head. She couldn't do that, and not because Ellen was off on her cruise. She loved Mia. She loved Nick. And he and the twins were a package deal.

Ava summoned an Uber ride and crossed her fingers that this would fall under the no-show exception for family emergencies. Otherwise missing the final was an automatic fail for the course.

———

Several hours later, Nick rushed into the recovery room. He'd driven like a madman from Boston after he's listened to the voicemail Maggie left him. Ava sat by Mia's gurney, her head in her hands, "What happened."

Ava lifted her head, her face white and her eyes red. "She broke her leg in two places doing a back flip off a picnic table. She landed wrong."

A backflip. Like he'd done showing off at his aunt's party.

"The medical team was taking her in for surgery on her broken leg when I got here." Ava sniffed. "By the time I signed the consent, I didn't really get to see her, reassure her. They said she should be waking up anytime."

"I'll sit with her. Would you take my rental car and pick up Lucas?"

"I can do that, but I'll take an Uber and keep Lucas at my place overnight. They're not going to let him in to visit, and you'll need the car if they release Mia in the morning as the surgeon said they might."

"Thanks for coming here, keeping Lucas, knowing I'd want to stay with Mia. Everything."

"No problem."

Nick attempted a smile. "By the way, how was your exam?"

Ava stood ramrod still. "I didn't get to my exam. Maggie called me about twenty minutes before it started. I came right here."

Nick saw red. "You didn't have to miss your exam. Didn't Maggie tell you that I'd given the club and her as manager permission to secure any necessary medical treatment if I couldn't be reached, like I've given you."

"She didn't say anything about that. I would have come anyway to be with Mia. Not that I really got to be. I'm going to see if the university will allow this as a family emergency and let me make up the exam."

Ava's reference to Mia, to them as family fanned his love for her. He reflexively reached for her. She inched back.

"Later," she said, looking around the busy room.

While his heart ached for her in his arms, he respected her wishes. "Later." He stared at the exit long after she'd left. If only there was something he could do to fix Ava having missed her exam.

"Mmm." A groan from Mia finally pulled his attention away from the door. The little girl's eyes fluttered and closed again.

Nick pulled the chair Ava had been sitting in

back next to the gurney and stroked Mia's cheek. "Uncle Nick is right here."

A minute later, Mia's eyes opened wide. "Uncle Nick. Where's Ms. Ava?"

"She went to pick up Lucas." He'd have to tell Ava that Mia did know she was with her.

"Thirsty," Mia said.

"I'll get a nurse for you." Nick strode over to the nearest person in scrubs. "My niece, Mia, Mia Cornwell, is waking up and wants a drink."

When the woman turned to answer him, Nick saw from her name tag that she was a doctor, not a nurse. "Mr. Cornwall?"

"No, Jansen. Nick Jansen. I'm Mia's guardian."

"I'm Dr. Natali, the pediatric orthopedist who operated. Nasty break, but everything went by the book. I'll be over to talk to you in a couple minutes. You can give her a small sip of water."

"Okay thanks."

By the time the surgeon had talked to him and Mia was moved and settled into a room in Pediatrics, Nick was ready to collapse. Mia was wide awake and chatty.

"We'd better call Lucas and Ms. Ava and tell them I'm all right. Lucas is probably worried about me."

Knowing Lucas, Mia was probably right. "Yes, we'd better." He'd planned to call Ava anyway, but later when they could talk privately. Before he could call Ava, his phone buzzed with her phone number. "Hi," he said.

"Hi, Uncle Nick. It's Lucas. Ms. Ava said I could call you."

Nick compartmentalized his disappointment in hearing Lucas's voice, not Ava's. "Hi, sport. Do you want to talk to Mia?"

"Yes!"

Nick handed the phone to Mia and leaned back in the bedside recliner, where he'd be spending the night. Eyes closed, he listened to bits of the kids' conversation from Mia's side.

"Yeah, it hurt a lot. I went to sleep, and it didn't hurt anymore. The doctor said it might hurt again tomorrow, but not as much." Mia lifted her sheet and peered under it. "Yeah, I have a cast. A pink one. You can sign it first. Then Uncle Nick and Ms. Ava. And the doctor said I'm going to get a scooter. One I can ride inside and outside. I'll let you try it."

Nick dozed off for a minute to thoughts of what Mia could do inside on a scooter.

"Mostly it's noisy. And it smells funny here. No, no ice cream. Okay. Bye."

"Wait," Nick sat up.

"What?"

He reached over and took his phone from Mia. "Nothing." He wanted to ... should ... call Ava back to let her know how Mia was. But Ava had to be exhausted. She'd done so much for him today. Her exam meant so much to her and her plans. The right words to express how sorry he was wouldn't come. Calling would just be disturbing her. He could survive an evening without hearing her voice. *Just barely*. He stuffed his phone in his pocket and turned to ask Mia if she'd be okay while he went to get something to eat. She'd gone from wide awake to fast asleep.

He leaned back in the chair again. Something to eat meant getting up and making his way to the cafeteria. After his four-hour mad drive home and the stress of everything, sleeping sounded like a better option. He pulled the blanket the nurse had brought around him and thought about ways for him to thank Ava. It had to be big. Something as meaningful as what she'd done for him.

"That's it," he mumbled just before sleep overtook him.

16

Ava awoke early the next morning to self-doubts. Maybe the fact that she chose Mia, Nick, her private life over her exam and her potential career as an attorney was a sign that her family was right. She wasn't cut out to be a lawyer. Or a member of the No Brides Club, even though there was no bride element involved. Her relationship with Nick was too new to even be thinking that. She reached over to the bedside table to grab her phone to call her sister for advice and saw an email alert from her course instructor.

Her heart pounded. A response to the email she'd sent him late yesterday afternoon about a meeting to discuss her missing the exam. She opened it. He wanted to meet at 1:00. Nick had said

Mia would probably be released about 11:00 or so. Ava took a firm hold of her future. If Mia wasn't released and Nick wasn't back to take Lucas, she'd take Lucas with her to the meeting if she had to and let chips fall where they might for her doing so. After sending a reply that she would be at the meeting, Ava fell back into a troubled sleep.

About 9:00, Lucas woke her. He was all re-dressed in the clothes he'd had on yesterday, except for his shoes. She'd had him sleep in one of her t-shirts. "Are Uncle Nick and Mia home? I'm all ready, except I can't tie my shoes."

Ava hopped out of bed. "Not yet. The doctor has to come check Mia at 11:00, so they won't be home until at least 11:30," she said.

"That's eleven-three-O, right?"

"Right. So we'll have some breakfast, you can help me with the dishes, and we'll watch a video. Then, it should be time. Okay."

"Okay."

They were well into the video when Nick finally texted her shortly after 11:00 that the surgeon was running late because of an emergency surgery. Her first inclination when she'd seen the text alert was to text back, *about time*. After she'd read Nick's text, she'd almost shot back, *can't someone else release her?*

Instead, she'd breathed deeply several times before texting,

All right. Keep me informed. If you aren't back by noon, I'll take Lucas to the Kids Korner and let you know. That better solution popped into her head. I have a meeting with my instructor at 1:00 about missing the exam.

Will do.

How is Mia this morning?

Grumpy about wanting to go home, he texted back.

As she lowered her phone to the coffee table, her phone pinged again.

About your meeting, you've got this. He followed his encouraging words with a thumbs-up emoji.

"Was that Uncle Nick?" Lucas asked before she'd been able to fully absorb Nick's reassurance. The little boy hopped to his feet. "Are they home?"

She ruffled his hair. "Not yet. The doctor is late." She sucked her lips in and released them. "I have an important meeting about school. If your uncle isn't back in time, I'm going to have to drop you off at the Kids Korner."

The little boy's lips quivered. "Do I have to? By myself."

She hugged Lucas, "Only if *I* have to." The more

she'd thought about the meeting this morning, the more she saw that bringing Lucas along wouldn't help her cause.

When the time started inching toward noon, Ava left Lucas watching the video and changed for her meeting. When she came back in the living room, she started pacing and straightening things that didn't need straightening. She just decided to get out the vacuum cleaner when Nick texted.

Still no doctor.

Okay. I'll have to drop Lucas at the Kids Korner.

Good luck!

Thanks.

Ava got Lucas and herself out the door and to the club by 12:20, leaving her plenty of time to get to her meeting. His sad, but stoic face when Ava left the Kids Korner and the club stuck with her the whole way to campus and while she stood outside her instructor's office waiting for him to arrive.

"Ms. Lewis," her instructor said, tight lipped as he reached to unlock his office.

"Mr. Landry." She expected or, maybe hoped, for a warmer greeting after reading the instructor's email this morning. Her feeling had been that he was open to her reason, excuse, whatever for missing the final. But, then, lacking emojis or specific words, emails were essentially void of emotion.

"Close the door and take a seat." She sat in the chair in front of his desk, and he opened a file on the desk.

"Yesterday, I was sympathetic to your reason for missing the exam and was planning to present it to my colleagues this morning as a legitimate family emergency excuse."

Ava swallowed hard. Yesterday?

"However, your going over our heads to the dean—"

"The dean? I didn't." She slapped her hand over her mouth for interrupting.

"No, apparently, you asked your fiancé to talk with his uncle who is a college friend of the dean."

Her fiancé? Yesterday that assumption would have warmed her to her core. Today it fried her. How could Nick have done that? After all that he professed having faith in her, in her abilities. "Peter Jansen?" she got out.

"Yes. I'm sorry to inform you that, despite your academic ability, you are not the caliber of person we want in our program."

Ava's stomach twisted until she had to grit her

teeth in pain. "No appeal?" she asked grasping for straws.

"Not for this year."

"I see." Ava fled, not caring what that behavior said for her. The weight of all she'd lost because of Nick was too much. She just had to get out of the office, off the campus. Not being in the NYU class this fall meant the cost and effort of reapplying all over again for next year. Reapplying for the scholarship sponsored by her kindergarten teacher and only having it for two years, instead of the three years of law school—if she even received the help again after having to turn it down now for this school year.

It also meant the end of anything between her and Nick and contact with the twins.

———

With the twins in the bedroom napping, Nick could hear every footstep in the hall. And every time he heard a footstep, he moved to the edge of his seat in the recliner to jump up for Ava's knock. He couldn't believe his luck last night when his uncle had called him to say the athletic club corporation's sale was a definite go. When Nick had filled him in on everything that had happened yesterday, his uncle said the NYU law school dean had been his college roommate, and that he'd put in a good word for Ava. That's what family was for.

The knock, more of a bang, finally sounded at the apartment door. He swung it open. "So should I order us all dinner in to celebrate. Maybe some ..." He saw the expression on Ava's face and bit back the *champagne for us for later* that had been on the tip of his tongue.

"Only if you're celebrating my getting kicked out of the law school class because of you."

Nick frowned. "What? Uncle Pete?"

"Yes, but I'm much angrier at you than your uncle."

Nick closed the door and leaned against it, fearing Ava fleeing before he found out exactly what he'd done. He'd never seen her this angry, nor so vulnerable looking. He took a deep breath to stop his constricting lungs. "Uncle Pete was just helping family. Isn't that what family members do? I love you. So I couldn't say no to his offer or to anything that might give you more clout at your meeting."

"Right. Because I don't have enough clout on my own without you jumping in to rescue me. At least my family is upfront enough to not lie about doubting my ability.

"Wait. That's not it at all. I wasn't lying. I do have faith in you achieving anything you want. I trust you to make your own choices. Like you did when you chose to be with Mia at the hospital. I can't believe what you put on the line for me. You helped me so much that I couldn't not try to help you. I'm sorry my help blew up on you."

Ava seemed to shrink in front of him. "I accept your apology. I'm as much at fault as you. I let myself fall into the same fantasy I had with my engagement, believing what I wanted to believe, not what was true."

Nick pushed away from the door and stood steel straight. "I am not your former fiancé, and I don't know how many more ways I can say I do believe in you and will support you in whatever you want to do now."

"But without your *support*, I would still be one of the new fall law students. The instructor had been in favor of giving me a family emergency exception and letting me take the exam...until your uncle's call."

Nick rubbed his face in his hands. "I messed up royally. I don't know how to fix it. Come sit with me and talk. The twins are napping. We can work this out."

She shook her head. "The only people I need to talk with are the No Brides Club members. Get my head back on track and my focus strictly on my career. If I hadn't let the temp agency talk me into taking the childcare substitute positions, instead of holding firm for law office positions, I wouldn't have left myself open to this *mess*."

"And you wouldn't have met me or the twins."

"True."

True. That's all she said was *true*. *Unbelievable*. Nick slapped the wall. "After getting to know you and meeting your family, I thought you were different, unlike my mother and the picture of family I grew up with. But I was wrong. You're a lot like my mother."

"If you mean a woman who knows her own mind and is willing to do what it takes to be successful in a man's world, yes I am."

"No, I meant like her in setting impossible expectations that no one could ever meet and refusing to consider the other person or find out who that other person really is. In that way, you're like both my mother and Constance, although *they* both seem to be mellowing with time."

Ava cringed, but didn't say anything other than, "I stopped by because Lucas left his video in my apartment. I figured he'd want it to take back to Philadelphia with you. I'd like to say goodbye to them before you leave."

Goodbye to the kids. Ava must feel she'd already said goodbye to him. "I'll see if we can fit it in."

Her eyes widened and her lips parted. She reached for the doorknob, keeping her gaze locked with his.

Nick knew he was being petty, but he felt petty. And if she was offering a stare-down, he was game. He'd faced a lot more formidable opponents than her.

Ava's lip quivered.

Or maybe not, as the motion went straight to his gut.

Before he could recover, she was out in the hall and closing the door behind her.

He almost reopened the door and went after her. No, after what he'd cost her, he'd better wait for her to cool down. He could take the kids to his house in Pennsylvania. Build the jungle gym he'd promised them. *Yeah.* Give Ava the weekend and then talk with her again. Hopefully, he could at least get them back to being friends. For the kids. For him. *Unless...* His windpipe constricted. He wasn't going to go to *unless*, not yet.

———

*A*va had gone home and blocked Nick's phone number. Her head pounded, and otherwise, she'd been too numb to talk with him anymore today. After taking a couple of aspirins and a restless nap, she dragged herself to her No Brides meeting, which was on the rooftop bar since it was such a nice evening. She ordered herself two Long Island iced teas before making her way through the afterwork crowd to the group's table. Tonight, it was all newbies like her.

"Hey," Marnie said when she reached the table. Vivian eyed the two drinks. "Are we celebrating or commiserating?"

Ava dropped into the last available chair. "Drowning my sorrows is more like it." She explained about the exam."

"So what's the game plan now?" Brooke asked.

Ava wanted to say hibernating for a couple of weeks until she had everything out of her system as much as she could. "I've called all the temp agencies I'm signed up with and specified law office work only. No, childcare gigs." She didn't say anything about Nick or the twins.

"Good for you," Samantha said.

She took a healthy gulp of her tea, then another. "Next, I'm looking at evening classes in social work, and applying to law schools again for next fall. I have the apartment sitting deal through the end of the year."

"It sounds like you dodged a detour and are getting things back in place," Emalie said, with the rest of the members murmuring their agreement.

Ava downed the rest of her first drink and started the second, as the other women rehashed their week, all of which sounded positive to her.

"Everyone ready to go downstairs and have something to eat?" Samantha asked when she wrapped up her week.

Ava polished off her second iced tea. All the positivity was getting to her. Not that the No Brides Club and the members' support wasn't exactly what she needed—all that she needed—long term. Short-term, she needed one more Long Island iced tea and to wallow in her own stupidity. Alone.

"I feel a headache coming on, so I'm begging off."

"You sure? Food might help," Marnie offered.

"No really. You all have been a lot of help. See

you next week." Ava waited until the women were on their way downstairs before she walked to the bar. "One more please." She sat in one of the bar stools.

"Can I get that for you?" A man, an attractive man, in a power suit asked.

Ava looked at him, then at the bartender through blurry eyes that had to be from the drinks. *They were not tears.* "Cancel that drink, please." She slid off the stool, turning her back to the man.

"I get it. You didn't have to be rude," he called after her.

Yes. Yes, she did.

Her head was nearly cleared by the walk home. What she saw when she pulled open the entry door to the apartment complex cleared it the rest of the way. Mia and Lucas standing with Maggie behind them, a hand firmly on each shoulder.

"Ms. Ava!" The twins easily escaped the other woman's grip to race to her and throw their arms around her legs.

Maggie shot her a poisonous look.

"We're going to see our new house."

Nick was moving home to Philadelphia already? Tonight, without letting her see the twins first, as she'd asked him? Anger, then hurt, flared inside her.

Maggie sidled over. "Nick's taking the kids to his

house for the weekend," she said. "He's loading the rental car in the garage."

"Yeah, Uncle Nick said you couldn't come because you have stuff to do," Mia said.

"But maybe next time." Lucas's hopeful expression tore at her.

"I'll have to see." Ava hated to be evasive with them. But she wasn't going to bluntly announce to the twins *and* Maggie that there wouldn't be any next time—although the woman might already know that.

"Nick should be bringing the car around any second," Maggie said with a Cheshire Cat smile that made Ava wonder if Maggie was going with them and if she was trying to get rid of her.

And Nick thought she was self-centered and scheming? Nick hadn't exactly said that. She sighed. And what she'd said to him hadn't been any better. Now was simply the wrong time for both of them. That's what she'd decided on the walk home, and she was sticking with that. Nick was getting on with his life, and she was getting on with hers.

"Here he is." Maggie grabbed the twins' arms and pulled them past Ava.

Mia twisted away. "Bye, Ms. Ava. See you when I get back."

"Bye Mia, Lucas. See you." She'd make every effort to see them before they moved—short of giving into that corner of her heart that wanted to go back to the day before yesterday. Ava turned and walked to the elevator, so she wouldn't see Nick, knowing he'd get out of the car to make sure the twins were safely in their booster seats.

The elevator pinged. Someday, after she was finished with law school and established in her career, maybe she'd meet another man like Nick, and have her own children.

A memory of his chuckle sounded in her head, mocking her.

Fat chance.

17

Ava's phone rang with a 716 area code. She ignored it. Wasn't the conventional wisdom that if you ignored spam calls enough, the callers gave up. She finished getting ready and picked up her phone to put it on do-not-disturb. The caller had left a message. Curiosity got the best of her. Ava pressed listen.

"Hey, it's Claire. I lost my cellphone and had to get a new number."

She hadn't talked to Claire in a couple of weeks, since the day Nick had sent the twins over with Ellen to say goodbye before he took them permanently to Philadelphia. After talking with Nick and finding out what he'd done, Claire had called her to see if she was okay. She'd lied and said she was fine.

The message continued, "I'm in Newark, meeting with the aunt and uncle of one of my minor clients and their attorney tomorrow morning about a possible placement with them. If you're not working, how about lunch? A college friend of mine has been hounding me to visit his new farm-to-table restaurant in Cherry Hill. I've got my car. Give me a call back."

Ava checked the time. It was only 9:30.

"Hi," Claire answered on the first ring.

"Hi. I'm not working tomorrow, and I'd love to do lunch. I need a break from the city, so Cherry Hill sounds great. What time? I can take the train, meet you at your hotel." *The half hour train ride, plus the twenty-minute walk to the hotel would give me something to do for the morning.*

"If you're sure, that would be great. How about 11:30?" Claire gave Ava the name of her hotel.

"Great. See you then." Ava hung up.

She slept better than she had in days. She didn't know if all the sleepless nights had finally caught up to her, or if it was the prospect of seeing Claire and getting out of her routine of taking every temp job she was offered and having the No Brides Club meeting as her whole social life. Despite her best intentions, she hadn't made any effort to visit any of the other sites in New York on her to-see list.

Ava pulled an Irish linen cotton double-breasted power suit she'd never worn from her closet. Kate had bought the classic glen plaid ensemble as a surprise gift to celebrate Ava's acceptance to NYU's law school. She squelched a shot of disappointment, by recalling all the support she'd gotten from the No Brides Club members since her exam debacle and her sister's fake-it-until-you-make-it creed for career women. Once she was dressed in the suit, accessorized with an oyster-colored camisole, a simple silver chain and earrings, and gray pumps, Ava felt empowered. If nothing else, Claire wouldn't be the only one overdressed for the restaurant.

Claire was waiting in the hotel lobby when Ava walked in.

"I love your outfit," Claire said.

"Thanks. I took lunch as an invitation to wear it, since I don't know when I'll have call to wear it again."

"It'll be before you know it," Claire said. "I almost changed into something more casual, but my meeting went over, and I didn't want to make you wait."

"Shall we go conquer lunch, then?"

Claire laughed. "You've got it. My luggage is already in the car. I figure it will take us a little over an hour to get to the restaurant. I made reservations for 1:00."

"Sounds good. I had a later-than-usual breakfast."

"How'd that temp job you told me about when we last talked work out for you?" Claire asked when they were in the car and on their way.

"Okay, if you like photocopying. I didn't know offices still did that when documents can be filled out and printed as many times as you want from a computer. It finished last Friday, and I haven't gotten anything yet for this week."

Claire told her as much as she could about her meeting without violating client privilege and caught her up on little Cole's latest accomplishments and the Jansen family, leaving—Ava thought—a gaping hole where Nick was concerned. Ava studied the suburban landscape as it rolled by. Leaving Nick out was probably for the best. She wasn't going to get over him completely if she got regular reports about him from Claire.

"Heard anything from Nick?" Claire asked. "He's miserable, you know."

So much for avoiding the topic.

"No." *I haven't heard a word from him, miserable or not. Nor do I expect to or need to.* "Do you mind if I read my email?" Ava said in case Claire was going to say anything else about Nick. "I haven't checked it since I got up and may have something from one of the temp agencies for tomorrow."

Ava took her phone from her purse and scrolled through her messages. Nothing she needed to respond to right now until she reached last message and saw the University of Pennsylvania Law School address. All air to her lungs was cut off. Feeling Claire's sideways glance at her, she clicked it open.

"Oh My God!" Ava shouted.

"What?" Claire said nearly as loud.

She sucked in air. "Penn Law. My first choice."

"What?" Claire repeated.

"I was wait-listed. They had a last-minute cancellation, and I was next on the list. I'm going to law school in three weeks."

"Con—"

"Wait." Ava held her hand up to Claire. "I have to send my response." Ava had so much trouble hitting the right keys on her phone that she'd resorted to one forefinger typing. She finished and flopped against the seatback. "There. You were saying..."

"Congratulations. Now we have something to celebrate at lunch."

"Thanks. I need to tell Mom and Kate." Ava texted them, saying she'd talk to them later, finishing as one of her favorite songs came on the radio. "Do you mind if I turn up the radio and bask in the sound and sun for a bit?"

Claire laughed. "Not at all. Bask away."

Before Ava knew it, they were at the restaurant. She drifted in on clouds.

"Yes, Jansen," Claire said when the hostess asked if they had reservations.

"You didn't take your husband's last name when you married?" Ava asked out of curiosity.

Claire looked startled. "I did. I don't know why I said Jansen when I made the reservation."

"Here you are. Back corner table." The hostess grabbed two menus. "Follow me."

She led them to the back of the room. Halfway to the back of the room, Ava plummeted from her cloud-bank of euphoria.

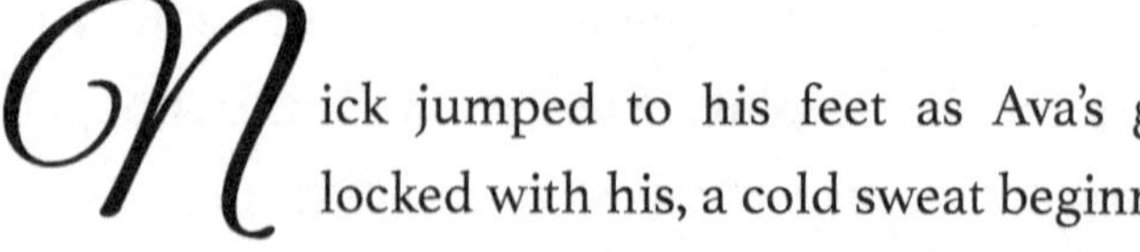

ick jumped to his feet as Ava's gaze locked with his, a cold sweat beginning between his shoulder blades and starting down his spine. While he tried to find his voice, he pulled out a chair and nodded toward it. "Was this your idea?" he finally got out.

"No," Ava said after a pause that seemed to go on forever.

"I set you up," Claire said. "You two are like a bad romance novel where the hero and heroine could solve everything by talking. So talk. Admit that you're both miserable, and whatever else it takes." She turned and marched toward the door.

"Where are you going?" Nick called after her.

"Home," Claire said over her shoulder.

Ava pushed the chair back under the table, as if to follow Claire.

The knots in Nick's stomach dropped like a dead weight. He put his hand over hers before she could let go of the chair.

It was now or never. "Sit. Please. I am miserable. I'm sorry that I acted before I thought and under-mined you. Love will make you do that, and other crazy things." He attempted his most winning smile to thaw Ava, who still stood gripping the chair.

Nick lifted his hand and she dropped into the chair.

"I'm miserable, too, and it's not all your fault. But

before we can move past this, I have to know that you understand why I was so angry and hurt."

Nick laced his fingers through hers on the table. "I have a good idea why but tell me anyway."

She curled her fingers around his. "It wasn't just that your action lost me my acceptance into law school. I knew I was risking that when I chose Mia over the exam. The way you went ahead and interfered..."

He cringed at the word interfered. But he had.

"...it made me feel that I wasn't up to defending myself, as my family has so often made me feel... Out of love, too."

"I was trying to do the family thing," he said with a dry chuckle. "Apparently, I need a few more lessons."

She squeezed his hand, making his heart leap with hope that he still had a chance to make things right between them.

"I need some more lessons, too, in seeing my own worth. The No Brides Club is a start, but I may need some private lessons in not being so defensive about accepting help."

She stroked the top of his hand with her thumb, sending his heartbeat out of control.

He stroked hers back. The soft expression his

touch brought to her face made him want to lean over and kiss her senseless. He'd already lost most of his wits. Why not her, too? But the restaurant was so public. He didn't want to ruin the progress they'd made.

"I might be able to fit those private lessons into my schedule. How's this for a start? You are as wise as you are beautiful."

Ava laughed, making her even more beautiful. "Corny, but I'll take it."

"Will you also take my word that I won't interfere in your career life unless you ask me to, or at the very least, I ask first?"

Ava bit her lip and nodded. "I can because I love you and know you love me." She waited heart pounding.

The light and look of relief Nick's smile brought to his face overwhelmed her. Ava grasped his hand with both of hers and leaned forward to kiss him. She stopped herself. One of the problems she had with getting others to see her as she wanted them to was her over-readiness to give in to her emotions. As much as she wanted to kiss him right now, she planned to have lifetime ahead with him to do that.

She cleared her throat, butterflies fluttering in her stomach. "Assuming you agree that we have a real thing between us and are presuming the lifetime ahead together that I am, I have one important parameter: We don't marry until I finish law school."

Nick sat silent so long, Ava wanted to disappear under the table. He'd never said anything about marriage. She swallowed hard. In her effort to keep her emotions in check, had she conversely let her them run ahead uncontrolled?

"Come here," he said in a thick voice, moving his chair close to hers and gathering her in his strong arms. "I love you so much, I could wait a lifetime for you. But don't ask me to."

"I won't." She lifted her face to him and invited the kiss she was bursting to give him. The restaurant, the people around them, thoughts of anything besides the feel of her lips on Nick's and how much she loved him disappeared. Until someone started clapping.

"Oh!" Ava pulled back.

"Did she say, *yes*?" someone called out.

"*I* said yes," Nick called, his thumb lifted in the air.

The other diners cheered, and a server arrived at their table with two luncheon specials. "Your friend who left ordered and paid for you." He placed the plates on the table.

"We'll have to do something nice for Claire to thank her," Ava said.

"Yeah, but right now all this serious talking has me starved." Nick dug into his lunch. After a couple of bites, he stopped. "That should hold me for one more important question. "What are your immediate plans?"

Ava placed her fork on her plate. "I'm moving to Philadelphia."

Nick dropped his fork. "You don't have to. Not for me."

"It's not for you." Ava was hard-pressed to keep her lips from twitching.

"Or for Mia and Lucas, if that's what you're thinking."

"It's not for the twins, although being close to you and them is a plus. It's for me. I've been accepted into Penn Law's September class."

"What? That's great."

"Yep, I was wait-listed, and they emailed me today that they had a last-minute opening if I was still interested. And before you ask, I'll be living in graduate student housing for the time being."

"I can live with that."

She and Nick finished their lunch between grins at each other.

"Do you want to go home, or can I talk you into coming to my place to see the kids," Nick asked as they finished their after-lunch coffee. "They ask me every day when they can see you."

"I'd love to see them and your house."

"And my mother?"

"Your mother?" The look on Ava's face was priceless.

"She's watching the twins for me."

"Your mother? With the twins?" Ava repeated.

Nick laughed. "Yes, she's mellowed some since we saw her at Aunt Sandy's party. It seems she ran into an old college friend at the Philadelphia airport on her trip home—male—and renewed their friendship."

Ava just shook her head.

"I'm not saying she's a totally changed person, but we're working on a relationship,"

"I'm glad." Ava said.

"Ready to go?"

"More than ready." Ava bit her lower lip. "There is one more thing I'd like you to do."

"Sure. What?"

"Come with me to the No Brides Club meeting on Thursday."

EPILOGUE

*A*va took her time walking to the Briarwood Tavern alone for the No Brides Club meeting. She'd dressed in the same outfit she'd worn for lunch with Nick. At her request, he'd be joining her —them—in a half hour, to give her time to explain things to the women. She rubbed her hands on her skirt and practiced what she was going to say. She wasn't abandoning the group. Like her sister, she'd be close enough to attend some meetings. And her relationship with Nick wasn't abandoning them either, not with his agreement not to press marriage until she'd completed law school.

She pulled open the door to the Briarwood dining room, where the club was meeting this week and made her way to their usual meeting spot without stopping at the bar for a drink. She needed her own courage, not the bolster of alcohol-enhanced courage. The room seemed emptier and quieter than usual. Maybe fewer members would be here tonight, cutting down on the potential critical judgement she feared.

"Congratulations," a chorus of women's voices said when she got within view of the club members. And from the ring of women who rose from their seats when Ava reached the group, it looked like all the club members and former members—or at least fourteen of the seventeen—some of whom she hadn't met before, were here. A cake decorated with a frosting mortarboard and diploma sat in the middle of the table.

"Kate." Ava took her sister to task. "This is your doing, isn't it? You said you couldn't make it tonight. You had to go to something with Jon." She looked past Kate to her brother-in-law seated behind her raising his beer to Ava.

"I fudged that a little. The something I had to go to with Jon was this,"

Ava hugged Kate. Luv you, sis."

"Hey, what's going on?"

A familiar deep voice behind her, paralyzed Ava. Nick wasn't supposed to be here yet, not until after she'd explained him, and everything to the members. She looked over Kate's shoulder, and his appreciative, loving gaze pinned hers.

Ava stepped away from Kate and the group. She didn't need to explain or apologize. Her and Nick's relationship was a small detour, but one she wanted to take and was prepared for. This was her life. She looped her arm around Nick's. He was her life. She was strong enough to be with him and be dedicated to her studies and her future career. If that meant giving up the No Brides Club, so be it.

"This is Nick," Ava said, "We—"

"We know," Kinsley, the club's founder said in a stern voice that made Ava's stomach drop and her spine stiffen.

Ava glared at Kate. She had to have told them. "I wanted to handle this myself," she said in a voice only Nick could hear.

He squeezed her arm and let go, stepping away.

A sensation of being cut loose in the wind vibrated through her until Nick stopped it by dropping to one knee and taking her hand.

"Ava will you make my life officially complete?"

he asked in a solemn tone she'd never heard from him before. Nick lifted a stunning solitaire ring he must have had hidden in his hand.

So much love filled Ava that she couldn't breathe, let alone answer. They'd informally pledged themselves at their lunch. This was so much bigger, more real. She'd never been happier in her life.

A cloud passed over Nick's face at her silence. "I promise not to say the M-word until you graduate from law school," he stuttered. "But I want you to know that I want you in my life forever, that I know you are my future."

She touched a finger to his lips. "I *know* I'll finish law school. I don't know if I can wait that long to be with you." Ava smiled. "I only committed to renting an apartment in graduate housing for six months."

"Is that a yes?" he asked.

She nodded to the cheers and clapping of her friends and let him slip the ring on her finger. His hand warm against hers. She tugged him to his feet. "Ye—" she started to say when his lips came down on hers, hungry and hard, and full of love. Her whole body singing, she had no option but to answer as hard and hungry and loving.

When they finally drew apart, her cheeks flaming, Nick whispered in her ear, "I'll love you forever,"

She whispered back. "I'll love you longer."

"I'll agree to disagree with that." Nick grinned. Now, did I hear something about cake? I'm starved.

Ava laughed. If possible, she loved him even more this second than she had a second ago.

WHAT'S NEXT?

**Read the first chapter of NO TIME FOR LOVE,
book 1 of the No Brides Club...**

The colors of dusk shot across the Manhattan skyline in vibrant magenta and tangerine, while the lights from the high-rise buildings twinkled like the first stars of the night. The view from the West Ridge penthouse was spectacular and added a bundle to the selling price. It also played a huge role in why her buyer wanted it, making it the largest sale in Kinsley King's career as a real estate broker. And that was saying a lot because she was among the city's best.

She didn't usually do walk-throughs this late in the day, but it was the only time the Sultan of

Mawta's representative could do it. "Everything you requested has been taken care of," she said, turning her back on the wall of floor to ceiling windows and strolling into the kitchen. The dark gray soapstone countertops had been replaced with white marble that had been highly polished to bring out the veining and character of the stone. That alone had cost a pretty penny, but the seller was willing to do just about anything to close on the property.

The tall, slim man ran his hand over the smooth surface. "Very nice. Exactly as requested."

Kinsley took him through the rest of the penthouse, letting out a sigh of relief after he left that everything was perfect. She'd been worrying all day that something might go wrong, but so far so good. Now they just had to get through the closing. It wasn't unheard of for a sale to fall apart at the last minute.

She needn't have worried, though. About an hour later, she was headed to her office in Tribeca, one of the most expensive neighborhoods in the city, with a nice big check in her hand.

"My, my, don't you look like the cat who swallowed the canary," Sue, her assistant remarked when Kinsley strutted into the office.

She grinned as she dropped the check on the

desk. "Nothing makes me happier than getting both ends of the deal, and this one has me ecstatic."

Sue's mouth dropped open when she saw the hefty commission seventy-five million brought. "Guess I don't need to ask if you're celebrating tonight."

"Looks like I'm buying dinner for the No Brides Club." Kinsley looked at her watch. "And I'm late."

"That's right. It's Thursday."

"Has been all day," she replied with a wink, before heading into her office to change into a sleek little black dress. Three years ago she'd met some fabulous women during Happy Hour at the Briarwood Tavern, an upscale restaurant with a gorgeous roof-top bar. Kinsley had been going there for years. It was her favorite haunt, especially after a stressful day of showings. She used to go alone, have a glass or two of wine while checking her emails, and then head home to her multi-million dollar loft on North Moore Street. However, now she had friends that were just as career-driven as she and who had dreams that didn't include a husband and kids. Many people would find that selfish, but those women didn't. They were all on the same page—tired of having their wants and needs pushed aside for a man's.

And that's why they formed the No Brides Club—a group of like-minded women who had sworn off marriage.

Kinsley took down from the closet shelf two evening bags—a Chanel and a Gucci—holding them both in front of her. She always had trouble deciding on accessories. Luckily, Sue didn't have that problem.

"What do you think? The envelope clutch or the velvet cross-body?" Kinsley stood in front of her assistant's desk.

"You know me. I'm a Chanel girl."

"Hmmm..." Kinsley handed her the cross-body, then tucked the black satin clutch under her arm. "You're right of course. Would you mind putting the Gucci back in my office? I've got to run!" She didn't wait for an answer. Sue knew the ins and outs of King Realty and was used to locking up.

The walk to Church Street was a short one, and Kinsley enjoyed the trek through the neighborhood with its cobblestone streets and cast-iron buildings. The nineteenth-century mercantile architecture was simple, yet beautiful. There wasn't the hustle and bustle of the Upper East Side, and that was one of the things Kinsley loved most about it. She spent a big part of the day in Manhattan and by nighttime was more than ready to return to the quieter streets of Tribeca.

When she entered the Briarwood, the usual Wall Street types were at the main bar. Kinsley had to squeeze past them, bumping into the back of a guy with a full glass of beer that nearly ended up all over her new Jimmy Choo shoes.

The group was at their usual table in the dining room, and she slid into one of the tufted leather banquettes beside Melody Mitchell, a pretty brunette with gorgeous green eyes. They'd met at a showing and had been at the bar celebrating Melody's new apartment the night they met the other No Brides Club members. Although they were a tight-knit group, Kinsley and Melody had become the best of friends.

"Sorry I'm late," she said. "I had a closing. Dinner and drinks are on me tonight."

"Well, then it's lobster and Champagne," Rachel, an aspiring Broadway actress said with a laugh.

Kinsley shot her a huge smile. "You go for it, girl. Tonight's a celebration. I'd been trying to sell the West Ridge penthouse for over six months and could've lost the listing if this deal hadn't worked out." With that said, when the waitress came by, she ordered a Magnum of Dom Perignon, after which she poured each woman a glass. "You all mean so much to me. I'm extremely grateful that you're part of my life." Kinsley raised her flute in a toast.

She'd just taken a sip when her cell phone rang. "No work tonight," she said, more to herself than anyone else as she ignored the call and set the phone to vibrate. A moment later it went off again and then again.

"Maybe you should take it," Melody advised. "It might be important."

"They're all important," Kinsley replied, letting it go into voicemail for the third time. "However, tonight I'm not working. This is my time with my girlfriends." She took a huge sip of champagne. Work was the love of her life, and most of the time she couldn't get enough of it. Kinsley was smart enough, though, to know that too much of a good thing could cause burnout. She knew when it was time to take a break and those breaks were usually Thursday nights at the Briarwood. But all good intentions came with a price, and that price could mean losing a listing, so a few minutes later, she excused herself and headed to the ladies' room where she checked her messages. The calls had come from an attorney in Upstate New York. Before she could call him back, her phone rang again. *Boy, insistent. Must be an anxious buyer. Her favorite kind.* "Hello. Kinsley King here."

"Ms. King, this is Robert Sykes, Cora Forrester's attorney."

Her pulse quickened. Why would an attorney be calling about her aunt? "Is Cora okay?" Her voice was high pitched and a little shaky, revealing her inner terror. Besides Kinsley's father, Cora was her only other relative. If something happened to her... Kinsley's thoughts were jagging in a million different directions and were interrupted by the man clearing his throat.

"I'm sorry. I hate to have to tell you this, but Cora passed away," he said quietly.

"What?" Her throat felt like it was about to close up. She swallowed hard, but that didn't help. A picture of the elderly woman's face appeared in her mind's eye—short silver pipe-screw curls encircled her round rosy face and her pale blue eyes, so much like Kinsley's mom's eyes. She'd never seen her aunt angry or upset. She loved life and had always lived it to the fullest, believing the cup was half full, never empty, even in her darkest of times. Kinsley had tried to emulate that in her own life but usually wound up failing miserably. There was no way she could match Cora's upbeat attitude.

She sucked in some much-needed air and then said in a small, squeaky voice, "What happened?"

She heard his heavy breath on the other end of the phone. "It was a heart attack. She's at peace. Remember that."

When Kinsley didn't respond, he went on to say, "You're her main beneficiary. I can mail you a copy of the will, but I think it would be best if you came here to read it. After all, there are the animals to consider. You're going to have to decide how best to run the sanctuary."

Kinsley's grief quickly turned to shock. "What do you mean, run the sanctuary?"

"Well, it's yours now. Although Cora did ask that Dylan Reese stay on as manager, she didn't make that a provision in the will, so ultimately it's up to you. If you'd like someone else, you'll have to let him go. Best to make these decisions right away."

"Yes. I suppose it is." Kinsley sank onto a plush velvet settee. "I have a few things I need to do in the morning. I can be at your office at one. Will that work for you?"

"That's fine. I'll see you then."

"Please text me your address."

"Will do, Ms. King. Good night."

After she hung up the phone, she held her head

in her hands and let the tears she'd been holding back flow freely. She hadn't seen her aunt in ages and guilt tugged at her heart. Kinsley should've gone to visit, but time had gotten away from her. There was always something important that required her attention, and that became even more the case after her dad retired and turned the business over to her three years ago. Still, she could've taken off a few days...

She thought back to when her mother died and how devastated she'd been. It was Aunt Cora who'd consoled her, despite having to deal with her own grief at losing her sister. Kinsley had spent a week at the sanctuary and during that time had grown even closer to her aunt as they celebrated Donna King's life, rather than despairing over the loss of it. That was seven years ago, and the last time she'd been to Forever Wild. She'd been amazed at how well Cora handled the animals, letting the wolves lick her face and the bobcats rub up against her. Kinsley had been terrified, but then she'd never even had a puppy. Animals weren't in her wheelhouse, but they were her aunt's entire world. And now she was gone, and Kinsley owned the sanctuary! A new wave of grief washed over her and with it another round of tears.

When the ladies' room door swung open, she quickly reached for a tissue from the box on the counter and began to pat at her face. She must look a mess with mascara and eyeliner smeared across her cheeks.

"Oh, my goodness, Kins!" Melody bent down to give her a hug. "What's wrong? We were worried because you've been gone a while. Does it have something to do with the calls you were getting?"

Kinsley shook her head. She opened her mouth to speak, but no words came out. When she tried a second time, she croaked, "My aunt died."

Melody sat down next to her. "Your Aunt Cora with the animal sanctuary?"

She nodded.

"I'm so sorry, honey."

"I have to go upstate tomorrow to meet with her attorney, and I've got so much to do before I leave."

Melody looked square in her eyes. "Just take care of yourself for once. The business will survive while you're gone."

Kinsley balled up the tissue and threw it in the trash. "You know that's exactly what my aunt would've said."

"She was a very wise woman."

She shot her friend a small smile. "She left Forever Wild to me."

Melody's eyes grew wide. "She did? But you don't know a thing about animals."

"Exactly, so not only do I have to deal with her death, but I also have to decide what to do with my inheritance."

Her friend's brows shot up. "Won't you just sell it?"

"That's obviously the most sensible thing to do. However, my head's pounding and I can barely think. Please explain to the others why I went home."

"Of course. But don't you want to take some food with you?"

"Just the thought of eating makes me nauseous. If I get hungry later, I'll make some soup." Kinsley reached into her purse for her wallet and then gave Melody more than enough cash to cover dinner and drinks for the women.

"That's not necessary," her friend remarked, trying to give the money back, but Kinsley refused to take it.

"I said it was on me and I meant it. Tonight was supposed to be a celebration, so I want you all to celebrate for me."

"I love you." Melody kissed her cheek.

"I love you too. We'll talk soon."

"If there's anything you need, just give a call."

"I will. Good night." Kinsley's thoughts were awhirl as she walked home. Images of her mom and Aunt Cora flickered through her mind, and it brought her some comfort knowing they were together in Heaven. But having been bequeathed Forever Wild was a huge problem and one she wasn't looking forward to dealing with. However, as she walked, the brisk night air helped to clear her muddled brain, and she knew there was only one thing to do. Sell the wildlife sanctuary.

What happens next?
Don't wait to find out...

Head to Amazon to purchase or borrow your copy of NO TIME FOR LOVE so that you can keep reading this sweet romance series today!

And don't miss Jean's NO TIME FOR APOLOGIES, book 5 in the series.

YOU MAY ALSO LIKE

Read the first chapter of FLIRTING WITH THE FASHIONISTA, book 1 of the CELEBRITY CORGI ROMANCES...

Ruby Ross pulled a freshly popped bag of kettle corn from the microwave and let the steam warm her face as she sucked it in the fragrant, buttery air with a contented sigh.

"Ahh, better than any spa treatment," she remarked to the fuzzy little dog squirming at her feet. She and her corgi, Diamond, had been together for almost three years now. Initially, she'd adopted the rambunctious little pup with the hopes that this new companion would help her get out into the city more—socialize, meet people.

But the tan and white corgi was far happier snuggled up on the couch than she ever was trekking through the sidewalk jungle of New York City.

Still, it didn't mean that Diamond was an easy dog to look after. She was forever demanding snacks, pets, and a four a.m. wake up time, and despite Ruby's increased exhaustion since adopting the discerning ball of fluff, she wouldn't trade her special girl for the world.

"Ready to start our party?" she asked the dog as they both made their way to the main living area of her studio apartment. Like everything else in this city, it was cramped to the max, meaning that both Ruby and her doggie roommate needed to use space efficiently and limit the number of personal items they kept. A small price to pay for being able to reside in one of the biggest fashion capitals of the world.

Diamond barked twice, then hopped up beside Ruby and attempted to swipe the popcorn bag from her hands with a quick nose and a pathetic whine.

"Stop that. You have your own." Ruby grabbed the dental bone from the drawer in the coffee table and tossed it over to Diamond.

The dog sighed and pushed the green chew onto

the floor, then started on a fresh string of barks. As much as Ruby didn't like being terrorized, she knew she'd need to offer Diamond something better if she had any hope of catching the pre-show red carpet coverage.

"You're in-*corgi*-gable. You know that?" She chuckled at her own joke as she fished a bully stick from the top shelf of the kitchen cupboard and tossed it Diamond's way.

Now she was satisfied. Good.

"Okay, but no more barking. You got it? This is basically the fashion Super Bowl, and this year I actually have a horse in the race." Yeah, she knew she'd mixed her metaphors, but Ruby was far too excited about fashion and far too uninterested in sports to care either way.

This was it, the big show and her first real chance at getting noticed by the fashion bloggers, reporters, and Hollywood's most respected stars.

Time had passed in a colorful whirl ever since acclaimed director Millie Sullivan had called on Ruby to design the perfect red carpet look for this year's Academy Awards. Millie, like Ruby, wore a size sixteen and said she wouldn't trust anyone else to dress her curves right. Doing so was especially important, considering that she was up for the best director award for the first time ever—and Ruby was so proud of her for the accomplishment.

Together they'd designed the perfect floor-length red gown with a high slit up the side and meticulous beadwork along the neckline. It seemed most in the industry expected bigger girls to merely "dress for their size," concealing their figures in simple black frocks while all the skinny girls topped off the best-dressed lists.

Ruby, however, had a different philosophy.

Celebrate your body as it is, because no *body's* perfect—that's what she often said when discussing her work with potential new clients or business relations. And that's what she'd told Millie, too.

Ruby's breath caught the moment she spied her newest showstopper on the red carpet. Millie was perfection personified with a bold red lip to match the gown and a perfectly coifed 1940's updo.

"Who are you wearing?" one of the reporters called, rushing over and waving his mic in Millie's face.

Millie looked straight into the camera like the practiced pro she was. Normally, she stood behind the scenes, but tonight she stole the whole show as she smiled wide and exclaimed, "Ruby Ross!"

"Oh, I haven't heard of her before," the reporter

gushed as he made a big show of examining her from top to bottom and back again. "But she does beautiful work."

"Yes, she sure does," Millie agreed, bobbing her head and showing off that bubbly personality Ruby had quickly come to love. "She's an up-and-coming force in the fashion world for sure."

"Honey, ain't nothing 'coming' about it." Turning to the camera, he added, "Ruby Ross, your star has arrived, and she looks fabulous."

Ruby screamed and stomped her feet on the floor, drawing an aggravated groan from Diamond, who was still making slow work of her prized treat. Well, not even a moody corgi could spoil her mood tonight.

"Did you hear that, girl?" she squealed. "Our whole life is about to change! Just you wait!"

Diamond picked up her bully stick and retreated to the bedroom, leaving Ruby to marvel at her good luck all by her lonesome. It didn't matter, though. All that mattered was that her work had been seen at one of the very biggest venues in the entire world. It had been noticed and then admired.

This was the big break she'd worked so hard for but had begun to doubt might actually ever come.

This was it.

And she was more than ready for whatever came next.

———

*B*randon Price's cell phone buzzed with an alert quickly followed by a second. Apparently he'd made the "worst dressed" list, and his father wasn't very happy about it.

Of course, he hadn't even wanted to attend the stupid awards ceremony, anyway—let alone wear a monkey suit to the thing. But when the gushing up-and-coming actress had begged him to be her date for the evening, Brandon's father had wasted no time accepting on his behalf.

That was the thing about dear old dad.

He saw his son as an extension of himself and his business rather than as his own person with his own dreams and ambitions. Price Sr.'s fitness empire had hit the big time when Brandon was still in elementary school. That meant moving to a larger, swankier house, switching to a private tutor and—worst of all —being groomed as his father's successor from a very early age.

While Brandon could appreciate the big muscles and flirtatious women that came with being heir to the popular health and fitness brand, he'd never actually gotten the chance to figure out where his own interests might lie.

And it was starting to look like he might never get the chance, either.

He'd had zero interest in the flashy awards show last night. It was so long and so boring. And besides, he'd only seen one or two of the movies that were nominated. His father had said it would be good for Brandon's image to accompany the sweet girl-next-door type to support her director who had just been nominated for the first time.

And so Brandon went, but he refused to go quietly. He'd grown a few days of messy stubble and paired his tuxedo with a mesh undershirt and neon yellow bowtie, thus achieving the worst-dressed accolade today. Not that it really mattered, anyway.

For as much as his father liked to complain about Brandon's rebellious streak, any press was good for them—yes, even the worst dressed list. For years, his bad boy image brought the fitness fanatics in droves. Everyone seemed to think that Brandon was living the perfect life filled with women, money, and fame.

Well, everyone except for Brandon himself, anyway.

Money was great, provided you could spend it on the things you wanted. Brandon's father kept close tabs on what he spent, where he went, and with whom. He wouldn't even let his son eat a slice of pizza. for crying out loud! In addition to grueling daily workouts and a regular diet of protein shakes and detox teas, Brandon wasn't allowed to eat *anything* that had been even slightly processed or that might otherwise mar his carefully maintained physique and glowing complexion.

It wasn't just frowned upon. This rule had actually made it into his contract.

It was also a condition of his trust fund, inheritance, and salary all rolled into one. Misrepresenting Body by Price would dash his wages and could possibly get him fired if he managed to take things too far.

Sometimes he'd fantasize about grabbing a super-sized value meal from McDonald's and scarfing the whole thing down right in his father's face, if only to call his bluff. And if Brandon got fired, so be it. He'd never asked for this job, and he was pretty sure his dad needed him just as much—or even more than—Brandon needed him.

Unfortunately, he wasn't actually qualified to do anything else. He'd only ever been paid to smile, look good, and parrot back all the words his father's publicity team shoved in his mouth day after day. He'd gotten his high school diploma but never had the opportunity to attend college. Dad said Brandon didn't need an education when his entire future was being handed to him on one giant organic, non-GMO platter. *Yum.*

He glanced down at his father's text now and frowned.

What were you thinking wearing that? the message came, typed out in very unnecessary all-caps.

Can't talk, Brandon texted back. *Lifting.*

That would avoid the upcoming confrontation at least for a little while longer. Give his dad some time to calm down. Despite the older man's huge success, he was always angry these days. Ever since Brandon's mom had asked for a divorce about five years ago, Dad had turned all his attention toward ensuring his son could never follow suit.

It was exhausting being the center of his dad's universe, especially since they had so little in common. It was all so shallow, every last part of the life they both lived. And Brandon longed for a way out, though he doubted he'd ever find one.

It hurt when the gossip rags called him dumb, spoiled, or any number of other insults they so enjoyed hurling his way. In truth, they didn't even know anything about him.

But then again, Brandon also knew very little about the real him that lay hidden beneath all the glitz and glamor. He supposed the media could be right about everything. Even his father could be right what was best for him, as much as he loathed the idea.

Maybe he was just a shallow pretty boy like everyone said...

Then again, maybe he was meant to be so much more.

Brandon groaned and grabbed a heavier pair of weights from the rack. If he strained his muscles hard enough, eventually his mind would quiet down and let him enjoy the day ahead.

It was better not to think.

Just do.

Just live one day at a time.

Eventually he'd learn to be grateful for the life he had and would stop thinking about all the things he was missing... right?

Head to Amazon to purchase or borrow your copy of FLIRTING WITH THE FASHIONISTA so that you can keep reading this sweet romance series today!

The Sweethearts of Country Music

Six musicians come together to form an all-girl country band. But when love comes calling, will the ladies be able to balance their musical worlds with their romantic lives?

Holidays in Hallbrook

Welcome to Hallbrook, New Hampshire. A small-town filled with the unexpected, lots of love, and of course, a beloved dog to ramp up the excitement. Home is where love leads you.

Mommy's Little Matchmakers

For these moms, a second chance at love may need a "little" extra help.

First Street Church Romances

These sweet and wholesome small town love stories with the community church at their center make for the perfect feel-good reads!

———

HISTORICAL ROMANCE

The Pioneer Brides of Rattlesnake Creek

Their fortunes lie out west...and so do their hearts.

Sweet Grove Historical

Go back in time to follow the lives and loves of Sweet Grove's founding families in this historical romance series.

COZY MYSTERY

Pet Whisperer P.I.

Glendale is home to Blueberry Bay's first ever talking cat detective. Along with his ragtag gang of human and animal helpers, Octo-Cat is determined to save the day... so long as it doesn't interfere with his schedule.

Little Dog Diner

Misty Harbor boasts the best lobster rolls in all of Blueberry Bay. There's another thing that's always on the menu, too. Murder! Dani and her little terrier, Pip, have a knack for being in the wrong place at the wrong time... which often lands them smack in the middle of a fresh, new murder mystery and in the crosshairs of one cunning criminal after the next.

The Funeral Fakers

Professional Mourning can be a deadly business. Luckily, these 6 out-of-work actresses are on the job!

Texas Sized Mysteries

The stars at night are big and bright, deep in the heart of Texas... but so is the trouble. These cozy mysteries feature characters who are larger than life and cases just begging to be solved by any reader clever enough to rise to the challenge.

MORE FROM JEAN C. GORDON

INDIGO BAY

(Each is a standalone story)

Sweet Entanglement (Sweet Romance Series)

Sweet Horizons (Second Chance Romances Series)

———

TEAM MACACHEK

Fall in love with the strong women and fearless men of
the motocross circuit

(Each book is a standalone story)

Mending the Motocross Champion

A Team Macachek Christmas Anthology

(Three Heartwarming Stories in One)

Holiday Escape

A Team Macachek Christmas

Christmas Pizza to the Rescue

———

UPSTATE NY . . . where love is a little sweeter

Bachelor Father

Love Undercover

Mandy and the Mayor

Candy Kisses

Mara's Move

———

LOVE INSPIRED

Bridges

Reuniting His Family

A Mom for His Daughter

The Donnelly Brothers

Hometown boys make good...and find love

Winning the Teacher's Heart

Holiday Homecoming

The Bachelor's Sweetheart

———

THE MATCHMAKERS ANTHOLOGY

A Match Made in Williamstown

ABOUT THE AUTHOR

For sweet romance author Jean C. Gordon, writing is a natural extension of her love of reading. From that day in first grade when she realized t-h-e was the word the, she's been reading everything she can put her hands on. Jean and her college-sweetheart husband share a 175-year-old farmhouse in Upstate New York with their daughter and her family. Their son lives nearby.

www.ingramcontent.com/pod-product-compliance
Lightning Source LLC
Chambersburg PA
CBHW021100110726

47900CB00007B/1965